D0005441

Georgia Rules

Georgia Rules

NANCI TURNER STEVESON

HARPER
An Imprint of HarperCollinsPublishers

Georgia Rules
Copyright © 2017 by Nanci Turner Steveson
All rights reserved. Printed in the United States of America.
No part of this book may be used or reproduced in any manner
whatsoever without written permission except in the case of
brief quotations embodied in critical articles and reviews. For
information address HarperCollins Children's Books, a division of
HarperCollins Publishers, 195 Broadway, New York, NY 10007.
www.harpercollinschildrens.com

Library of Congress Control Number: 2016960400
ISBN 978-0-06-237457-8 (trade bdg.)

Typography by Erin Fitzsimmons
17 18 19 20 21   PC/LSCH   10 9 8 7 6 5 4 3 2 1
❖
First Edition

For Mom—with love and admiration

ONE

On a hot day in June, when all I wanted was to come back from my run and cool off in my room alone, Mama didn't even give me two minutes recovery time before she sent my world spinning. I was late for lunch, still sweaty, probably smelling like the locker room of a high school football team, and was counting on her to send me off to shower before being allowed at the table. She barely glanced my way. Instead, she wiggled in her seat and cleared her throat twice, then stood up so fast her chair almost fell backward.

"My word, what good is central air-conditioning if it

doesn't keep you from sweating like a bronc on rodeo night?"
She nervously adjusted the little lever under the thermostat
on the wall, then sat down again and fanned herself with her
hand. "I grew up without air-conditioning, did I tell you that?
And believe me, it's a whole lot hotter where I come from than
it ever thought about being here in Atlanta!"

More sweat broke out on my brow. The wiggle-and-throat-
clearing thing was a sign she was about to drop some kind
of bomb. I took a sip of sweet tea and swiped a napkin across
my forehead. "Yup, you told me."

She shifted one more time and before I even had a chance
to catch my breath, she laid the biggest kind of crazy ever
right in my lap. "Did I happen to mention your daddy left you
his farm in Vermont when he died?"

My daddy had been dead almost four months. I figured
there must be something wrong with me because I never felt
the type of devastation you're supposed to feel when a parent
dies. It's not like I knew him that well. Mama had been married to Peter since I was five, and some days I forgot about
my daddy altogether. I don't think I even cried. When my
best friend Irene's dog died, I was near inconsolable for days.

"No, you didn't tell me," I said. "I mean about the farm."

Mama picked up her salad fork and pushed lettuce around
the plate. "Well, he did. Those kind of things always take
time, but we finally got the formal documents. I had the
lawyer check everything out. It's all official. There's even a
trustee. And guess what else? We're going to live there for
one year."

That knocked the air right out of me. She might as well have said we were moving to Siberia. Or Montana.

Her face puckered up like it did when she'd been dipping into her not-so-secret stash of Sour Patch Kids candy. "What are you looking at me like that for?" she asked.

"I'm waiting for you to tell me what you mean."

"About what?"

"About moving to Vermont. Does Peter want to go?"

Then she pretended to be really invested in her soup, stirring, sipping, studying mint-colored ripples that spread to the painted meadow around the edge of her bowl. "Oh, he's not going. Just you and me. It will be like an adventure."

"And Peter's not going becaaauuuse . . ."

Pause.

"Because he's decided to divorce us, that's why."

Then she did look at me. Right square in the eyes. And because of what I saw in hers, I didn't let the hissy fit loose that was simmering just under my skin. She was scared. I took a deep breath and picked up my spoon, drawing in the creamy sensation of chilled soup, letting it coat my tongue and hoping it would have the same soothing effect on my spinning brain.

"Peter's decided he likes that friend of his, Albert, better than us, so we're moving out and Albert's moving in. If it weren't for the opportunity your daddy's farm gives us, I might feel like discarded furniture. But I don't. Now stop acting so shocked and close your mouth—it's hanging wide open."

My mouth wasn't hanging open because she'd implied my very proper stepfather was gay. It was hanging open because I couldn't imagine—if it was true—how he'd kept that a secret for so long. He and Mama didn't approve of homosexuality. Or at least, that's what they'd always said to me. One time at dinner, I told them about a discussion some friends and I were having at school about gay marriage. Mama had been so horrified, she'd leaned in to me and whispered, "We don't discuss things like that, sugar." Then she'd made me give her the names of all the other kids, and she'd actually called their parents.

That was my least popular week at school.

"Well, you can go to Vermont if you want," I said. "I'm staying in Georgia." I turned back to my lunch, signaling that my decision was final.

"And just where do you think you'll live?"

"Here. With Peter."

Her nostrils flared. "You, Peter, and Albert? Not a chance. We're going to Vermont and there is nothing more to discuss." She sat tall and lifted her chin, signaling that *her* decision was final.

"Why can't we stay in Atlanta and just live somewhere else? We can find an apartment near my school."

"Do you have any idea how much that fancy school of yours costs? How do you expect me to pay for something like that?"

"Peter will still pay for it," I said, my bravado fading. "Won't he?"

"He's not throwing us to the dogs, if that's what you mean.

He'll give us enough to live on, but I can't hold my head up in this town anymore, not with this—this dark shadow of shame being cast over my head."

She waved her salad fork around in the air.

"Two divorces, one from a man not right in the head, the other from a man who's decided he's in love with another man, and I'm only thirty-three years old! No, this is our chance to start over. You and I are going to Vermont and that's final."

Now it was my turn to wiggle. "But we are coming back after a year, right?"

"How can I answer that right this second? You always want answers to the most impossible questions when I'm stressed, do you realize that?"

I wasn't thirteen yet, but even I knew the truth. Any question was impossible when Mama was like this. It didn't matter if I asked how her day was, or what the astronauts on Apollo 13 ate for breakfast, it would be too difficult for her to answer. So I shut up.

"All we need to think about right now is getting through the year. It was in your daddy's last will and testament. One year, then we can sell the place and have a huge amount of money to live on the rest of our lives. Those four thousand acres are worth a fortune. That's the *only* reason I'm taking us back there."

"Well, I'm the one in school, so I vote we stay here."

"Until you are an adult, your vote doesn't count. So get over it and start packing."

* * *

Peter didn't come home until after dinner. I figured he'd planned it that way on purpose because he knew Mama was going to tell me about the divorce. Once inside, he made a beeline for his study, but he left the door open. That meant it was okay to interrupt. He sat at his computer examining a colorful graph on the screen, his back tall and stiff, his starched shirt buttoned to the top, his hair clipped in precise half circles over each ear. It was the same way he sat at the breakfast table, the same way he sat in his car and in the stadium at my track meets. I knocked gently.

"Come in," he said.

I perched on the edge of a leather chair and clasped my hands together, hoping it made me look calm and relaxed on the outside. Inside, things were stormy.

Peter swung around. "Did you know Thomas Jefferson invented the swivel chair?"

I nodded. "You showed me when we went to Monticello."

"Yes, I'd forgotten. I did."

I shifted uneasily. The speech I'd spent the afternoon preparing escaped out the top of my head like dandelion seeds blown away from the stem.

"I suppose your mother spoke to you?"

"Yes."

"I hope you don't judge me too harshly."

"No."

He dipped his head in a teeny-tiny nod and his eyes softened, like he'd really been worried I would judge him.

"I'll always see to your finances. You and your mother won't suffer for funds, and if you ever need anything, you can always call me. You know that, right?"

Then I remembered what I came to tell him. "I don't want to go to Vermont."

Silence.

Maybe he didn't understand I needed his help to make that happen.

"Can you tell her to stay? I don't mean in this house, but here, in Atlanta. I don't want to move."

Peter's left cheek twitched, just under his eye. He folded, then unfolded his hands. His cheek twitched again, and I knew right then that he wasn't going to help me.

"I understand," he said. "I really do. But she's thinking of your future. It is best."

My future? What about now? What about this very minute?

I waited, hoping he might say something else, something with more promise to it. But he didn't. Nothing. We stared at each other until his computer screen turned dark in power-save mode.

"Okay," I finally said.

"I'm glad you understand. We'll talk more before you go."

"Okay."

Peter reached out and touched my shoulder with his fingertips before turning back to his computer. I left the room feeling shocked and defeated. Really, who moves from the busy city of Atlanta to a town in Vermont so tiny you've

probably never heard of it, right smack in the middle of summer, when your best friend is an ocean away on vacation and
you can't even say good-bye to her?

Me. That's who.

TWO

After four long, lonely days in Vermont, we still didn't have internet. We didn't even have cell service, because living out in the boonies meant we had to have some special machine to draw in satellite signals. And I still hadn't ventured outside the big, rambling farmhouse to explore the property that was supposedly now mine.

All of the above made me cranky. At breakfast, Mama made it clear I had to change my attitude and get on with life.

"You're depressed," she said, jerking the hot sauce bottle so hard it made a red pool in the middle of her grits and burned my nose from across the table. "I am, too, but we have to deal with our current lot in life. It's only for one year. A person can do almost anything for a year, if they put their mind to it. So put your mind to it and get outside. You're pale as a ghost."

She reached out to touch my cheek, but I pulled away.

"All you've done is lie in bed for four days and read those books of yours. Get outside. Run," she said. "That always fixes you right up."

She was right. Running was the only thing, besides losing myself in a book, that guaranteed happiness for a while. After lunch, I headed outside, fully intending to start by running a mile. I didn't get very far. Instead, I stopped at the threshold of a big red barn on the property. I was scared to go inside. On the drive up north, Mama'd said my daddy had lived and died in that old barn. I wasn't sure how literal she'd been, but what if his ghost was still lurking around, waiting for me to show up?

I put my face close to a gap in the door and cocked my ear, listening for who knows what. The only sound came from the wisp of falling dust. That's pretty darn quiet.

"Magnolia Grace?"

I launched a foot in the air and landed looking in the other direction, my hands up in front of my face. A man with skin as dark as midnight stood about ten feet away, with a black and brown dog sitting on its haunches by his side.

"Oh! Who are you?"

He took a step closer and put his hand out like he wanted

to shake, then changed his mind and stuffed it back into the pocket of his jeans.

"I'm Deacon. I live over there in the caretaker cottage," he said, indicating a small building tucked into the edge of the woods. He reached down and scratched behind the dog's ears. "And this is Quince. She and I have been watching over the place for you since your father passed."

My nerves jangled. Mama hadn't said anything about some man living on the property. That didn't mean he was lying—half the time, whatever Mama said could be all lie, part lie, or shaded truth. But you'd think she'd have told me something this important so I didn't get spooked, like I was right then.

"Does my mama know you're here?"

He nodded. "She does. I'm sorry if she didn't mention it. I didn't mean to scare you."

"How did you know my daddy?"

Deacon smiled, and when he did, a tingling sensation dropped over my head like a veil.

"Oh, that's a long story. I don't want to interrupt your visit to the barn. You go on in. We can talk another time."

I looked through the gap in the door and shook my head. "I'm not going in there. It's creepy."

"Suit yourself," he said. "That barn isn't going anywhere. Part of it is on the historic registry." He jerked his chin toward the house. "I think your mama might be looking for you."

Sure enough, Mama was watching from the porch of the white clapboard house, hands on hips, her hair already done up all blond and big. She was wearing a pair of supertight black leggings, a hot-pink polo, and drippy pearl earrings. She looked completely out of place.

"Guess I'd better go inside."

Deacon nodded. "We're right over there if you need anything," he said, indicating the cottage. "Teakettle is always on."

"Yes, sir, thank you."

I started across the gravel driveway, checking to see if Mama was mad I'd been talking to a stranger. We weren't allowed to do that in Georgia.

"Magnolia?"

I turned back. "Yes?"

"Is that what they call you? Magnolia? Or your full name, Magnolia Grace?"

"No one calls me Magnolia. I'm Maggie."

"Maggie," he said. "Okay, Maggie it is. But just so you know, to your father you were always Magnolia Grace."

At lunch I sat by the big kitchen window looking out to a grassy field that sloped gently away from the house. A crooked wooden gate hung from a fence going across the yard. Wildflowers dotted the field in no particular order—yellow and pink, orange and fuchsia, with an occasional stalk of something blue mixed in. The field stopped abruptly at the edge of a forest scattered with tall trees with white bark.

The view was so different from the manicured lawns and bordered azalea gardens I'd known back home. Atlanta felt so far away. Mama was silent while she set our food out.

"Why didn't you say anything about that man Deacon who lives here?" I asked.

She ignored me and grumbled something instead about the house not having a proper dining room. It really bothered her, even though the kitchen was twice as big as the one back home and had enough room for two dining room tables. Plus, it had an actual fireplace in the corner, made from blue-gray stones, with these black hooks inside to hang pots from, like they did in the olden days. I'd never seen a fireplace in a kitchen before.

"He lives in that old building on the other side of the barn with his dog, Quince. Have you seen it? The shed? Or cottage, I guess he called it. They call stuff by different names here, I think."

She sat down with a plunk and laid a paper towel across her lap. "Now, how would you know if they have different names for things? This was the first time you were even out-side the house."

It wasn't really a question, so I didn't answer. Instead I bit into my chicken salad sandwich, put together the same way our housekeeper, Clarissa, made it back in Georgia, with chopped apples and pecans.

"Do pecans grow in Vermont?"

No answer.

"I could look it up myself," I said. "Well, if we had internet I could. Why is it going to take so long for the cable people to come?"

"Because that's the way things happen in the boonies," she said. "I can assure you, if I'd known there wasn't even a TV in this house, let alone internet, I would have made arrangements long before we left. And to think people say Southerners are slow."

"Why do people say Southerners are slow?"

Mama picked at her bread crust. "Sugar, did you wake up today and decide to ask a year's worth of questions I don't have answers to? Because that's the way it feels, and I'm not in the mood. I've got a lot on my mind right now and would appreciate a little sensitivity to my needs."

Mama's needs were always requiring my sensitivity. I grew up understanding that her needs were first and foremost in our lives. Mine came second. Or third. Or tenth, depending on who else was around at any particular moment. I shut up and studied a flock of birds that rose together out of the tall grass and flew away in unison, disappearing over the tops of the trees. A little something lonely tugged at my heart.

THREE

After lunch, Mama tried to get me to go with her "in search of civilization."

"You aren't the only one going through real-life withdrawals. Only place I've been in four days is the grocery store. I need to see people. Real, live people. Come with me. It'll do you good, too. We'll go exploring."

I weaseled out of it by saying I didn't get to run yet, since I'd gotten delayed when I met Deacon outside that barn. The truth was, I wanted to scope out all the stuff left behind in the house without her hovering and making snide comments about my daddy's family. As soon as she peeled out of the driveway, I walked from room to room, trying out mismatched chairs and sitting on an ancient couch that was so stiff it could have been used as a diving board.

Portraits of my ancestors hung everywhere—ancestors I'd never even known about. Mama said the pictures were coming down the minute the movers brought our stuff from Georgia. She didn't like them all staring at her—said it made her feel judged. "They're all so stuffy," she'd complained.

I lifted one from the wall and checked the back. Along the bottom, written in faded ink, it said *Alexander Austin, 1879.* Most all of them had legible writing and were lined up around the rooms in order of year, starting with Alexander on the wall below the staircase and ending with Micah in the front hallway. But none of those people smiled. Not one. It was the most unsmiling family I'd ever seen.

Upstairs, in my room, was the only photo I had of my daddy. It was taken when I was about six, the year after Mama and Peter got married, and the only time my daddy came to see me in Georgia. We'd been at some kind of fair with a carousel. My daddy stood almost as tall as the pole coming out of the middle of the horse I rode—white, with a flowing pink mane and tail, and a golden saddle. He'd wrapped his giant hands around my waist and held on while we went around and around. After the ride was over, he paid a photographer for two copies of the picture he took of us and gave one to me. The other he'd tucked inside his shirt pocket. I'd slipped mine inside the waistband of my shorts and walked carefully to my room when I got home so it wouldn't fall out. Since that day, the picture has lived in the one place I knew Mama would never look—inside a book.

I got that photo and carried it around the house, holding it up next to each of the sketched portraits, trying to compare the people on the walls to the man in the photo. It was hard to tell if there was any likeness. It was even harder to see anything of myself in those people. I happened to like smiling.

There was only one portrait in the front room, which Mama called a "parlor" and had ruled off-limits to me. She said the furniture in there was valuable, and if we got in a pickle about money, she could sell something to tide us over. But once I opened the doors and saw that lone portrait hanging over the piano, I had no choice. I had to go in. That person was smiling.

Ever so carefully, I lifted the carved gold frame from the wall and checked the back. *Benjamin Austin, 1942.* He looked more like my daddy than any of the others, partially due to the mass of wild hair springing from all over his head, and partially because he smiled like he had a secret. That one time my daddy had come to Georgia, Mama'd made a big deal after he left about the way he'd let his hair grow "all long and shaggy." In my shadowy picture, his eyes were focused downward, on me, but his mouth curved up into a tiny smile, like he was pleased with himself for something no one else knew about.

Looking at the two of them, my daddy and Benjamin, my

heart did that little drop thing, the same way it did when I had to leave Atlanta without saying good-bye to Irene. Maybe I was finally feeling some sadness over his passing. Maybe I wasn't flawed after all. And maybe, while I was stuck here in Vermont, I could learn a little something about him and eventually even have a good cry.

FOUR

Unless you happen to like to sweat—which I do not unless it comes after a good run—spending July outside in Vermont is a lot nicer than swimming through the humidity that suffocates Atlanta, where I sweltered every year from March until Thanksgiving. But now I found myself drawn to the front porch early each morning by cool breezes and the chatter of a million different birds singing in the field and trees.

Mama rarely got up before ten, so the only other early morning sound came from Deacon's truck rumbling down the driveway when he and Quince left. The quiet made my insides calm in a way I never remembered feeling. It was a nice break from the constant hubbub of living in a big city. There were a couple of times, when a colorful bird flew by or the sweet scent of the baby-pink flowers growing in the yard floated past my nose, that I thought it was a shame to have to give up this place at the end of the year. It might be nice to get away from Atlanta and come sit on this breezy porch every summer.

About two weeks after we arrived, a mail truck sputtered and chugged up the long driveway and stopped in front of the house. The mail guy got out and carried a white envelope with red and blue stripes to the door. Mama must have been on the lookout for him. It wasn't ten o'clock yet, but she was up and waiting. She flung the door open, snatched the envelope from his hand, and slammed the door shut without saying a word.

The man looked at his clipboard and grumbled, then raised his hand to knock.

"Wait!" I said. "I'll sign."

He turned to look where I was sitting on the porch swing. "Oh, I didn't see you theyah—can you sign for her?"

He talked funny. I walked across the porch and reached for the pen.

"I'm her daughter—is that okay?"

"Just sign theyah," he said, pointing to a line at the bottom.

I figured "theyah" meant "there," so I scribbled my name,

then went back to the swing while he squinted and studied my signature.

"We have different last names," I said.

"Ayuh, I sorted that out. What's your name?"

Was I supposed to give a stranger my name, even if he was the mailman? He tapped his pen on the clipboard.

"I need to know so I can print it."

"Oh, right. Maggie Austin."

"M-a-g-g-i-e Austin," he said, writing it out as he spoke. "Ah, that makes sense. You must be Johnny Austin's daughtah."

Johnny Austin's daughter.

I was Johnny Austin's daughter. That's the first time I remembered ever hearing someone say it like that. I pushed the floor with my toe and made the bench swing rock again.

Johnny Austin's daughter.

"Well, welcome to Vermont, Maggie Austin. I'm Jeffrey. Your dad was one of my favorite people. He didn't get out much, but we had some good talks heyah on the porch, when I could catch him."

His mouth twitched into a half smile. I sat still, like a mute, until finally he did a little wave and trotted off down the steps.

The next morning Mama was up early again. I heard her making noise in the kitchen before nine and went in to find her with her nose inside a shiny green bag of coffee.

"One thing I'll say about Vermont, they do sell some fine coffee," she said.

She scooped some grounds from the bag and dumped them into a filter, poured water into the back of the coffeemaker, and turned it on. The smell of java filled the kitchen.

"And what are you up to today, sugar?"

Her cheerfulness this early was unsettling. "I want to go to the library. Can you take me?"

She got her mug from the cabinet and examined the inside, like she expected a spider to crawl out. "Library? What do you want to go to a library for?"

"I'm tired of sitting on the porch every day. Besides, I happen to like books, remember?"

"You brought books, *remember*?"

"I don't have any about Vermont. If we're going to be stuck here a whole year, I want to learn about things. Like those trees out there in the woods. Why do they have white bark?"

"Now how would I know that?"

"Exactly. And since we don't have the internet yet—"

"Internet, internet, internet," she said. "I want it as much as you do, but can't you think about something else? What do you think people did before the internet, little missy?"

I stared at her, not believing she'd walked herself right into that trap. "They went to the library, and they read books."

"Psshhh," she said, flipping her hand. "I can't take you today. I have an important errand on my agenda. You'll have to suffer through another day on that porch."

"Where are you going?"

She poured coffee into the mug, then placed her palm against my cheek and smiled. "I'm not telling. It's a surprise. A going-away gift to us from Peter."

"I don't feel like surprises."

"Well, I don't feel like arguing, and since I'm in charge of us, I win."

Two hours later, Mama waved playfully as she pulled out of the driveway. I gave her the hairy-eyeball look and pushed the porch swing so hard with my foot I thought the rusty old chain holding it up might break. Wouldn't that serve her right, coming home to a daughter lying on the front porch, tangled up in a bunch of chains, all because she wouldn't take her to the library.

FIVE

The next morning Mama still wouldn't tell me what her supersecret errand was the day before, but she did agree to drive me to town. We passed the library three times before realizing that the yellow house on the corner with baskets of pink and purple flowers dripping all over the porch railing was not someone's home but actually the address we'd been looking for. Back in Atlanta every library looked the same: low gray buildings and cement walkways, automatic revolving doors and security cameras pointed at the entrance. The front door of this library was propped wide open.

Mama scanned the three-story house and rolled her eyes. "Small-town America at its finest." She handed me a white envelope. "You'll need these to get a library card. I'll be back in an hour."

She drove away with the windows down and music blaring. It wasn't like Mama to drop and run. I couldn't decide if I felt dumped or free. After she turned the corner, I walked up the steps and past two white pillars and baskets of green ferns, then stopped short, startled by the words on a simple bronze plaque hanging next to the open door.

TOWNE LIBRARY, AND THE BOOKS WITHIN, WERE MADE POSSIBLE THROUGH THE GENEROSITY OF JOHNNY AUSTIN AND ARE DEDICATED TO HIS MEMORY.

My Johnny Austin? My eyes moved left to right. I read the words over and again, but each time they said the same thing. My daddy had donated a library to this town. An entire library. What kind of kid doesn't know that about her own blood relative?

I stalled, giving myself a second to ponder this before going inside, when a large, boisterous family swarmed up the steps behind me, chattering and laughing, completely unaware I was in their path. There wasn't anything I could do but get shuffled along with them until they split up and left me standing in a room unlike any library I'd ever imagined.

It was like being in the middle of someone's living room, someone who loved books and comfortable places to read. Colorful sofas and chairs were grouped around coffee tables decorated with little vases of fresh flowers and framed photographs. In between the floor-to-ceiling bookshelves, tall, thin windows shed light everywhere. There was not one tubular, headache-producing fluorescent bulb to be seen. And the books. So many books my fingers quivered.

The sweet smell of leather binding and flowers, and the homey feel of the library, made me forget about the plaque outside. I scouted out the first floor, a large, open area, with the exception of a circle of desks in the middle of the room. A wide staircase in the back led one flight up. The second floor felt more like a regular library, with row after row of bookshelves in one giant room, and people hunched over computers on two narrow tables at the far end. Internet!

A lady who was restocking shelves looked up and smiled at me. "Can I help you?"

"Yes, ma'am. Am I allowed to use the computers to go on the internet?"

"Sure," she said. "Use your library card downstairs to reserve a time. They're full right now, but maybe in an hour."

"Thank you."

She turned back to her cart. If I got a card now, I'd have to hand over all my identification papers. If someone made the connection between my name and my daddy's, they might ask me a bunch of questions I didn't know how to answer and I'd feel stupid. I wasn't ready to feel stupid. I wanted to explore.

I started up another staircase that took me to the kids' section on a third floor. A room to the left had a sign that said Teen and Young Adult. The room to the right had one that said Picture Books and Early Readers. But above me, in the middle of the ceiling, was a glass dome made from dozens of small windowpanes, each one framed in white wood. Sunshine and blue sky spilled through the glass. Tips of leafy branches surrounded the edges, making a green snowflake pattern around the border. I gaped at it with my head tilted back, wondering why every building in the world didn't have a window on the ceiling. It was so beautiful.

A man came up beside me and cleared his throat. His name tag said his name was Jeremy.

"Oh, hello," I said.

"You've never been up heyah I take it?"

"No, sir, I haven't."

"It's a beauty, that one, ayuh? He was a masteh."

He sounded like Jeffrey the mailman—times ten.

"Excuse me?"

"The ahh-tist. The one who painted it."

"Painted what?"

He raised his eyes to the ceiling. "Up theyah."

I tipped my head back and looked up at the glass dome and the sky.

"You thought it was real, ayuh?"

"It's not?"

Jeremy motioned for me to follow. "Look heyah."

He pointed out a window. Clouds had moved in and dappled the air. Everything that had been blue before was now that in-between lavender color that happens when rain clouds get between the earth and the sky. I went back to stand underneath the bright blue dome again and squinted.

"The leaves are all different, and they don't move. That's how you tell," Jeremy said.

He was right. Not one leaf breathed. Each one was a unique example from different trees. In just the few short weeks since I'd been in Vermont, I could already make the distinction between a heart-shaped birch leaf and a lobed oak.

"Who painted it?" I asked.

Jeremy smiled and turned his palms up. "Local ahh-tist. Same one as donated this place. Johnny Austin. Bit of a recluse. Died in the spring. Tragedy."

I stared up at the ceiling and shuddered.

SIX

I did want that library card after all. I had to get on the
internet and do two things: get in touch with Irene and
do a search for Johnny Austin. My feet barely touched the
stairs as I raced to the second floor, gripping the envelope so
tight it scrunched in the middle. Just as I hit the last step, a
redheaded boy with a cart full of books stopped right in front
of me. I grabbed the bottom of the banister with both hands
and tried to stop my momentum, but the lower half of my
body flung around and slammed into his cart.

Books took to the air like startled birds. My hands ripped
from the wood and I landed with my face planted on a copy

of *Journey to the Center of the Earth*. The boy stood over me, holding tight to the cart, his mouth twisted into a humiliating smile.

"I'm so sorry," I said. "I didn't see you."

"Apparently."

He reached his free hand out to help me up, but instead I crawled on the floor, gathering books as fast as I could, and stacked them in piles on the stairs.

"You don't have to do that, I've got it," he said. "They'll be in the way there."

He was right. The towers of books in the middle of the stairs made for a surefire booby trap. He waved his hand as if to say I was free to keep moving, but I couldn't stop staring at his red, red hair. I'd never seen anyone with hair that color. Pomegranate red, not carrot orange.

Mama's voice whispered in my ear. *Don't gape, it's unattractive. We don't do that.*

Impulsively, I held out my envelope. "I'm going downstairs for a library card."

A woman as thin as a willow branch rushed over and snatched the envelope away before the boy could take it.

"I'll help her," she said. She let a little puff of air escape from her lips and looked at me. "You have to have an adult sign you up. James isn't eighteen yet."

James rolled his eyes and grinned.

"Sorry," I said, pulling myself up.

Library Lady wiggled her finger. "I'm Miss Hilly. Follow me."

Downstairs, she spread my personal papers all over a desk right smack in the middle of that big room where anyone could walk up and read them. She studied each page from top to bottom, eyed each photo ID suspiciously, and checked the way I looked now against a four-year-old passport photo from when we'd gone to Greece. She squished her eyebrows together, then peered back at the papers. You'd think I was applying to work at the CIA.

A couple of people lined up behind me, their arms loaded with books.

"Magnolia G. Austin," she said thoughtfully. "Are you related?"

There it was. I kept my arms straight at my side and gave her a blank expression.

She shook her head. "No, of course not. One minute."

What did that mean, *Of course not*?

Miss Hilly scrunched, then unscrunched her forehead. Her fingers slowly click-click-clicked on the keyboard. She twisted her mouth funny, bent down to get close to the screen, checked one of my documents again, then finally reached into a little machine and pulled out a brand-new green and white library card.

Magnollia G. Austin, it read.

With two *l*'s.

She'd misspelled it. For real. She was a librarian, and she'd misspelled my name. I handed it back to her.

"I'm sorry, but *Magnolia* only has one *l*, not two," I whispered.

"What?"

My face flushed. "Yes, ma'am, one *l*."

She put the card close to her face, then shrugged. "Look at that—let me do it again."

This time she typed slower than cold honey dripping from a spoon, checking each letter before tapping the key. The line of people behind me grew longer. I could feel their eyes boring into my back.

"Magnolia G. Austin," she said.

Each time she said it, the people in line got more restless. We'd been at this now for at least fifteen minutes. A cranky kid wound himself up into a full-blown tantrum. His mother put their books on one of the coffee tables and left.

"What's the *G* for?"

"Grace," I whispered. "You can just put Maggie, if you want. Maggie with two *g*'s."

"No, no, it has to be the same. Magnolia," she said again. "Like the tree?"

I'd never had this much trouble with something so simple as a library card in Georgia. Of course, back home Mama would have come inside and handled the whole thing herself. The new Vermont Mama was tossing me from the nest rather abruptly.

"Yes, ma'am."

Someone behind me giggled. Library Lady grinned like we were best friends. "Don't listen to them. I think your accent is adorable."

Finally, *finally*, she handed me the card. I turned and barreled out the door. I didn't want to get on the internet anymore. All I wanted was to hide until Mama came to pick me up. And more than ever, I wanted to be back in Atlanta where I knew what to do, where no one cared about my name, my accent, or my father.

SEVEN

The next day a yellow moving van made its way slowly up to our house. The driveway wasn't that steep, not like a giant hill, but it was long and in one spot curved sharply to the right. In the elbow of the curve, a fat old oak tree looked like someone had taken a giant razor and scraped off a bunch of bark, exposing the flesh in the exact spot where a car might come too close. The driver was trying hard to avoid leaving streaks of paint on the tree.

Mama ran from the house, trotting down the steps, saying, "Oh, thank God, thank God" to herself, as if the perils of living without her own belongings had almost sent her to an early grave. She ran right past me and waved her hands frantically, directing the driver to pull close to the front porch. I have to admit, I experienced a flicker of excitement myself, knowing my own pictures and pillows and the rest of my books would be here. But on the heels of that came a vision of Mama ripping down the portraits and replacing my ancestors with stuff Peter had let her take from the house in Georgia. Stuff that didn't mean anything.

I ran inside, slipped into the parlor to grab Benjamin off the wall, and lugged him all the way upstairs to my room, stashing him in the back of my closet.

"Sorry, Benjamin, it's only temporary." I moved a flattened box in front of him so no one peeking in my closet would see that I'd hidden him there.

The movers finished before lunch. Mama's cherry-colored love seat sat in the center of the huge family room, like a tiny neon light in the middle of the Arabian desert. The mismatched chairs and hard couch had disappeared. Stacked boxes created paths for us to move between the rooms.

"We'll deal with all that stuff later," Mama said from the kitchen. She unwrapped china plates as gently as one might unfold the petals of a daffodil. "Look, sugar, our things are here."

I'd never paid much attention to Mama's attachment to "things" before, but right then it really bothered me. It wasn't like the china had been passed down from her grandmother. It was all stuff Peter let her buy with his credit card. It could

be replaced as easily as it was purchased, unlike the paintings of my ancestors.

"What are you going to do with the portraits?" I asked.

Her face clouded over. "Something. I don't know. I don't
care about them today."

She smiled at a gold-rimmed saucer and put it on the
counter next to her set of those little tiny cups people use
to drink that really strong coffee. Mama said that stuff was
thick as mud and tasted like the bottom of a horse stall, but
she always made sure those cups were brought out of the
cabinet when company came for dinner.

"Maybe the library would like them," I said.

"Okay."

She hadn't even heard me.

"Because my daddy donated the library to the town, so
maybe they'd want them."

"Good." She set a creamer and sugar bowl on the counter.
"Maybe they'll come pick them up. You can ask next time
you're there."

I got up close to her face. "Did you even know he donated
that library?"

She looked at me like I was silly. "Your daddy did all sorts
of crazy things, sugar. It doesn't surprise me one bit. If you
want them to go to the library, that's fine. They're yours.
Otherwise they're going to live in that barn until next July
when we move, because decorating is my department."

Deacon and Quince stopped by that afternoon with an envelope for Mama. "This is for August," he said. "Thought you
might want it early."

Her eyes flashed and her whole body stiffened. She glanced
quickly at me, then stuffed the envelope inside a drawer and
slammed it shut.

"Thank you."

For all her proper manners, the one thing Mama never
could control was the way she changed when someone humiliated her. I had no idea what Deacon might have done, but it
didn't matter. There was no reasoning with her when she got
like that in her head. That icy voice of hers gave her away.

"Is there anything you need help getting moved? Any
boxes you want me to take upstairs?" Deacon asked.

She turned her back to him. "We're fine." Short, clipped
words.

"Okay, if anything comes up, you know where I am."

Mama rolled her eyes. "Indeed we do."

"Wait!" I said. "Can you help me?"

Mama's head flew up. "With what?"

"Moving the portraits to the barn."

She stared like she had no idea what I was talking about,
even though we'd just had the conversation a few hours
before.

"They'll be out of your way," I said quickly.

She shrugged and cut a straight line with a knife across
the top of a box. "Suit yourself."

There were seven portraits, not including Benjamin, who might be suffocating up in my closet. I brought each one to the front porch, and Deacon carried them across the yard with Quince trotting at his heels. When he came for the last one, I followed them all the way inside the barn.

It was dark and cool in there. The smell of turpentine and something sweet lingered in the air. The whole middle was empty, just a broad floor made from smooth, creamy stones. Two wooden sawhorses and a bunch of rusty tools leaned against a wall. Near an opening in the back, a blue tractor faced out to the field, with clumps of green grass clinging to the wheels. Patches of sunlight pushed through dusty windowpanes, spreading streaks of yellow across the stones.

I tilted my head back and followed a three-quarter walkway around the second floor, turning a full 360 degrees. It felt like standing in an old church, one where God had been waiting for me a long, long time.

"I like it in here," I whispered. "I like it a lot."

Deacon watched me, still holding the last portrait.

"It's like I should remember," I said. "We lived here for a few months when I was little. But I don't remember this place."

"Not everything needs a visual memory," he said. "Sometimes moments come to us by smell or sound or even taste."

He leaned the picture against a wall near the others, then climbed a staircase and returned with a tarp. "I'll get boxes tomorrow and move them upstairs. They'll be there whenever you decide what to do with them."

"Thank you," I said. "I'm sorry Mama was rude."

He shrugged. "It's okay. She'd rather be in charge of her own money, but I'm the trustee. It's my job to see to it things are done according to the way your father wanted."

"*You're* the trustee?"

"I am."

"I thought a trustee was someone official, like from a bank, or a lawyer. Not just a regular person."

Deacon laughed. "Glad to know I'm regular. I've wondered for a long time. A trustee just means I handle the aspects of your father's estate where you and this farm are concerned. Your mama will either get used to it or she won't. But don't worry about me."

I walked slowly back to the house, thinking about what Deacon had said. Feeling obligated to another person humiliated Mama, and when Mama was humiliated, she lashed out. That mean streak of hers had embarrassed me more than once in my life, like the time a new track coach chewed me out in front of all the parents for getting a bad grade, which meant I couldn't compete. Mama'd lit into her so fierce that woman could probably still feel the burn. But, like she had told me, living in Vermont was only for one year. A person can do almost anything for a year.

That night, while Mama was in the shower, I wrote a quick letter to Peter. I wanted to let him know we didn't have internet yet, in case he was wondering why I hadn't emailed. On the last line I said, "We have an extra bedroom, just in case you and Albert ever want to come visit." I wrote out his name and our old address on an envelope and ran down the driveway in my slippers to put it in the mailbox and flip the little red flag up. Just to be safe, I'd stuck four stamps across the top so it would go fast, all the way to Georgia.

EIGHT

A few days later that redheaded boy from the library came strolling up the driveway, leading a mule and trailed by a bunch of girls in assorted sizes and colors. The second I saw that flash of red hair against the background of green trees by the road, I leaped from the porch swing and made a mad dash for the front door, hoping to disappear before he caught sight of me. No such luck.

"Look, James, there she is!" One of the girls had spotted me.

James smiled and waved. How the heck did he know where I lived? Now I had to be polite. I started over to meet them, but stopped short at the bottom of the porch steps when I saw a shiny stick thing stuck to his leg, making him limp.

"Hi, Maggie with two *g*'s," he said.

I couldn't answer. I just couldn't, because it wasn't something stuck to his leg, there was no leg. I hadn't noticed at the library when he was wearing jeans, but now, in shorts, I saw he was missing part of one leg from just above where a knee should have been.

A chunky girl with thick bangs cut straight across her forehead watched me staring.

"I don't think she's ever seen someone who lost a leg before."

I forced my eyes to move to James's face. Two girls on the back of the mule snickered, and heat rose up my neck. I wished I'd agreed to go with Mama to pick out paint colors. I even wished she'd come home right then. I'd have to help her carry the buckets into the house, these people would have to leave, and this awkward moment would be over.

"I'm sorry, I didn't mean to stare."

James hadn't stopped smiling. "It's okay, it's not really lost."

All four girls giggled.

"It's not?"

"Nope, I know exactly where it is," he said.

"You do?"

"Yup. Buried in the backyard alongside two cats, one guinea pig, and Rugby. That was our dog. He died right after we buried the leg."

The girls laughed together. I hate that feeling, being the odd one on the outside looking in. It was the same way Irene made me feel when she wanted to be mean, which happened whenever her big brother was nasty to her. The two girls slid off the mule's back and stood with the others. I wanted to run inside and never come out again.

"Buried?" I sounded like a frog croaking.

James sat down in the grass and unbuckled the silver thing from his thigh. A black sneaker poked off the other end.

"Take a look," he said, holding the whole contraption out. "Go ahead."

I shrank back and crossed my arms over my chest. "That's okay—thank you anyway."

The chunky girl took the leg from James and knocked her knuckles just above the sneaker. "It's titanium. It's really cool."

"Oh, I see."

She passed the leg back to James and thrust her hands on her hips. "You're Magnolia Grace."

I nodded. "Yes, I am."

"Well, I'm Biz and I have two moms."

Nothing—ever—in any of Mama's manners lessons I'd endured over the years could have prepared me for how to answer an introduction like that. Especially coming from a little kid who looked like she might be going into first grade in the fall. If so, this was no ordinary first grader.

Biz pulled another girl forward who looked a little older

than me. She was the exact opposite of Biz; tall, with straight black hair and large brown eyes that slanted slightly at the corners.

"This is my sister Sonnet," she said. "But she's not Portuguese."

Biz and Sonnet giggled.

A girl with tawny skin and wiry brown hair as wild as Benjamin's raised her hand. "I'm Kendra," she said.

Then the tiniest girl stepped beside James and studied me with clear, blue eyes under a mop of tight, yellow curls. James ruffled the top of her head.

"This is Lucy, the baby."

Lucy dug her elbow into his thigh. "I'm not a baby. I'm five and three quarters. I only look little because I was a preemie and my birth mother left me at the hospital so my real moms could come and get me."

Preemie? Birth mother? What five-and-three-quarter-aged kid knew those kinds of things, let alone said them out loud?

"And there's one more sister," Biz said. "Haily."

"She's at the store today," James said.

"She's 'working,'" Biz said, air-quoting the word *working*.

Kendra rolled her eyes. "Working means she's waiting for this boy to show up so she can flirt!"

"She has a bf! That means boyfriend," Lucy chimed in.

"The girls are more excited about him than Haily is," James said.

"Not me," grumbled Kendra. "Sonnet doesn't care either."

Sonnet nodded silently.

"What store?" I asked.

"Our moms own Parker's Country Store just this side of town. You'll get to meet them soon," said James.

"That's how we knew you were here," Lucy said.

My head flipped from one kid to another, settling on James. "Do I know them?"

"No, Deacon helps them at the store a few days a week," he said. "He told us back when he first found out you were coming."

Biz crossed her arms over her chest. "Yeah, but he said we had to wait for you to get settled before we came over."

Lucy crossed her arms like Biz. "Yeah. Settled means at least two weeks. Sometimes more, like with you."

Kendra nudged James. "We have to go."

Lucy and Biz started talking at the same time.

"Aren't you going to ask her?"

"It's getting hot."

"I'm itchy. I wanna go."

Lucy tried to yank off her T-shirt. James quickly pulled it down over her body. "Okay, okay."

"Ask her!" Biz demanded.

"We're on our way to the river to swim. Wanna go with us?"

And then I was crowded into the middle of a circle of James and the two littlest girls, who talked at the same time, telling me about the rope swing at the river, and who was the best swimmer and the worst, and all the reasons I should come with them, and how we could go to their house afterward and eat all the ice cream we wanted because their moms owned the store. Sonnet stood apart, watching us and scribbling something in a pocket-sized notebook.

"I'd have to ask and Mama's not home," I said, secretly relieved. There were so many of them.

"You say *I* funny, like there's an *a* with it," Biz chided.

Lucy elbowed her. "Shhh."

I didn't want to go with them. I didn't want to have to wait and introduce Mama to this strange family and see her try to hide her disapproval. She'd be real nice to their faces, but afterward, when it was just the two of us, she'd call them bumpkins. When she learned they had two moms, she might call them something worse. Mama's judgment of other people always made me feel *less than*, like I probably came up short in her eyes too.

But I didn't have a choice about asking or not because right then, a brand-new, fire-engine-red Mustang convertible spewed gravel under shiny black tires on the driveway and came to a screeching halt in front of the house.

Mama was back.

NINE

S he got out of the car, her head wrapped in a turquoise scarf, wearing sunglasses as big as the whole state of Georgia, and lipstick that matched the Mustang. When she saw all of us standing there, including the mule, she lowered her sun shades and raised her eyebrows. My stomach dropped to my feet. This was going to be awful.

"Is that your mom?" Biz could barely breathe. "She looks like a movie star!"

Mama made her way around the side of the car and sashayed across the yard, waving one arm in the air. "Well, hi, y'all! Sugar, do we have our first guests?"

Her pointy high heels sank into the grass, almost causing her to trip and fall. "Oops, silly me!" She slipped off the shoes one at a time and tiptoed barefoot toward us. "I hope that dog of Deacon's has its own private place for you know what other than in our grass!"

Lucy and Kendra giggled. Sonnet pulled the pencil from behind her ear and scribbled in the tiny notebook again. Biz's eyes popped.

"And she's so nice!" she said.

Wait for it, I thought. *Just wait.*

Mama stopped short when she saw James's leg. Or no leg. Or thing that was there instead of a leg. And she stared. With her mouth open. Just the way she'd always said made me look like trailer trash. I pleaded with my eyes for her to stop, but she didn't see because her attention was aimed only on the titanium stick attached to the black sneaker.

"Mama. Mama!"

She startled and looked around, like she'd just noticed all of them. "Oh! Excuse me."

"This is my mom, Mrs. Baird," I said.

She untied the scarf and pulled it off her head. Masses of wavy hair fell past her shoulders.

"This is James," I said.

He reached out and shook her hand. "James Parker, nice to meet you. These are my sisters."

The girls said their names one at a time. Mama looked from one to the other, her mouth slightly open and her eyes wide. "Y'all are all from the same family? Well, it's so nice to meet you. Isn't it nice to have new friends, sweetheart?"

"We came to see if Maggie wanted to swim," James said.

"And an invitation to swim, too!" she exclaimed.

That was not what I expected. First of all, I didn't know these people were already my friends. Except for Biz, I couldn't remember which sister was which. And second, shouldn't I be able to use the Georgia rules to my advantage on an as-needed basis? Like now? In Georgia, Mama would have to meet their parents before I'd be allowed to go off with them. She didn't even know about the two-moms part yet.

Mama plastered a smile on her face. "I didn't know there was a pool nearby. Is there a country club I haven't sniffed out yet?"

"Around here, families swim in the river," James said. Emphasis was on *families*.

Silence.

Mama looked from girl to girl, then right to James's leg without even stopping at his face.

"I see. Well," she said slowly, "my only problem would be there's no lifeguard at a river, and we're used to swimming under the supervision of a trained professional."

Maybe this was going to go my way. Maybe Mama would save me from an outing to a river with all these people I didn't know, who talked about things that were never even whispered at the country club. At least not in front of me.

"James is our lifeguard," Biz said.

"Yeah, James is our lifeguard," Lucy echoed. The other two girls nodded.

Mama's eyes focused on his leg again. "I don't—"

"I understand," James interrupted. "But I'm still a better athlete than most of the kids in my school. And I'm CPR certified."

Maybe Mama felt a little ganged up on. Or maybe she thought I wanted to go with them, because she let it go, right then and there.

"I suppose if you're certified and all, you ought to be able to watch over my precious for a swim in the river."

"Yay!" Biz high-fived me.

Lucy raised her china-blue eyes, which made Mama's whole face soften. "Is it okay if afterward we go to the store for ice cream?"

Mama bent down and got close to her face. "Well, aren't you just the most adorable thing ever? And what store do you mean, sweetheart?"

"We own the country store near town," James said. "Little over a mile up the road from here. Sue and Kori will be there. I can drive Maggie back if it's too late."

"Who are Sue and Kori?"

Here it comes.

"My moms," James said without hesitating. "We have two of them."

On behalf of this family who would now be judged mercilessly at our dinner table, I flinched. Visibly.

Mama's shoulders rose so slightly no one else probably saw it. But I did. I knew her body language as well as I knew the name of the hair color she used every month to keep her roots from showing.

"Two moms. I see. Is there a father involved?"

OMG. "Mama, that's none of—"

"It's okay, Maggie," James said. "We all have different fathers. Sonnet, Biz, and Lucy are adopted. Haily and I are from when our moms were married to husbands. Kendra is a foster."

When James singled her out, Kendra scowled and turned sharply away.

"And how many does that make altogether?"

"Six. Five girls and me. Haily's working at the store today."

"Is that so," Mama said slowly. She cocked one hip and pulled the scarf through her fingers, looking suspiciously at each of them, one at a time. Then she caught my eye. I don't know what she misunderstood about my expression, but she uncocked the hip, tied the scarf around her neck like a cowgirl, and said, "Well, James, all I have to say is that Vermont is a very interesting state."

Then she waltzed back across the yard, stopping at the new Mustang to gather her purse and shopping bags.

"I'll take you for a ride in the new car later, sugar," she called. "In fact, I'll take all of y'all! Isn't it exciting? I've waited my whole life for a red Mustang convertible."

She kissed the tip of her fingers and pressed them onto the hood of the car before disappearing inside the house. This time it was Biz's turn to drop her mouth open.

TEN

This recurring abandonment thing with Mama had turned annoying. I didn't mind when it meant I got to stay home alone for a few hours—which I never got to do in Atlanta because either Peter or Clarissa were always around—but this time I felt like she'd thrown me right into that river and walked away before waiting to see if I sank or swam. So, I did what Mama did in times like this. I lied, cool as a glass of iced tea on a scorching afternoon.

"My bathing suit hasn't come yet," I said.

Lucy tugged my hand. "You can swim in your underwear."

"Or not," James said quickly. His ears turned near as

red as his hair. "She doesn't have to swim."

Kendra yawned, big, like the whole idea of my coming with them bored her. "Maybe she just doesn't want to go."

"She's coming," Lucy announced. She slipped tiny, pale fingers into my hand and tugged. "The river is this way."

And just like that, off we went.

By the time we reached the road, the others had caught up and were happily gossiping about Haily's new bf. The mule's giant hooves made nice clopping sounds on the road, one-two, three-four, one-two, three-four. Lucy had a ginormous smile on her face, like she'd won me as a prize. And I was going to the river.

We crossed a field with pale grass so high Lucy could have gotten lost if she hadn't been holding my hand so tight. I think she was afraid if she let go, I would run back to the house to hide. She just might have been right.

Halfway across we stopped for the sisters to change places riding the mule versus walking. Lucy gave up her turn to hold me captive.

"Do you have a sister or brother?" she asked.

"Nope."

"Why not?"

"I don't know."

"Whaddya mean you don't know? You have to know."

"I guess because my daddy was away most of the time he and Mama were married."

"You don't have to have a father present to have a

baby—don't you know that?"

OMG.

James stared straight ahead and pretended not to hear. I stammered and stuttered, trying to think of what to say. Finally, I leaned down and whispered, "I still don't know why."

"Well, that's dumb."

Once the girls had switched places, James picked up the mule's reins and started walking again. "Look out, Maggie," he called over his shoulder. "She's a pistol."

"The mule's name is Molly," Lucy said. "Because a girl mule is called a molly and it's easy to remember. Did you know that?"

"No, but it makes sense."

"Did you even know this is hay growing in this field?"

"No."

"You don't know much about anything, do you?"

Kendra swung around and sat backward on Molly to face us. "It's already been cut and baled this summer, Lucy. This is the leftover. And stop being rude. She's new. You have to be polite to new people, remember?"

"She's not new," Lucy insisted. "She lived here before when she was little and now she came back. She was here before you, or me, or maybe even Sonnet, so there! Right, Maggie?"

Her expression was so hopeful, I couldn't tell her I barely remembered anything, so it really didn't count. I nodded just a tiny bit, hoping it was so tiny neither one of them would think I was siding with the other. No such luck. Kendra narrowed her eyes and swung around, turning her back to me.

The rest of the field crossing was uneventful, except when Molly raised her tail and deposited a big load of manure in my path. I squealed and sprang to the side, barely escaping my foot being planted in the middle of the hot, steaming pile. Biz laughed so hard she had to run ahead and find a tree so she wouldn't wet her pants. If it hadn't stunk so bad, it might have been funny in a welcome-to-Vermont kind of way, something I could laugh about with Irene later. But that mule's manure was so rank, I gagged.

After the long walk, the sight of cool water spelled serious relief, a reminder that I had ignored any form of cross-country training and was more out of shape than I ever remembered. The river looked fresh and clean. There was a sandy place on the bank, and an old rope with a knot at the end hanging from a tree leaning over the water. If I'd had my bathing suit, I just might have gone in. Next time. If there was a next time. I sat down against the tree and fanned myself with a small branch of leaves.

Biz's face looked like one of those cherries you get in a Shirley Temple, red and puffy. She blew the bangs off her forehead and stripped out of her clothes right in front of me, all the way to pink-flowered cotton underwear and undershirt. Her tummy stuck out, and her feet curved in awkwardly, the left foot more than the right.

"My feet were bunched up when I was in utero," she

announced, pulling a bathing suit on over her underclothes.

In utero?

She'd really just said that out loud? In Georgia, you never, ever discussed reproductive body parts outside of health education class. When I'd started my period, Mama'd handed me a book and a box of pads and asked if the teacher had already told me what to do. Even Irene and I never talked about the particulars, and we never, ever said anything about a woman's uterus. Mama said that was between a lady and her doctor.

Everyone stopped getting ready to swim and waited for me to respond. Finally, Lucy spoke up. "She doesn't know what that means. You have to explain things to her. She's like from another planet."

"I know what it means," I said. "I just—"

"Okay, okay, that's enough!" James clapped his hands. "Everyone in the water. Git!" He shooed them away and shrugged an apology.

"I do know what it means," I said.

"I know. This is what it's like to have a bunch of sisters, if you were ever wondering."

"Is that good or bad?"

He tossed his T-shirt into the grass, then sat at the edge of the river, still in his shorts, and removed the silver leg. "Neither. Just is."

Scooting down the bank, he pushed off into the water, the half leg kicking out just like the whole thing was still there. Biz and Lucy splashed and crawled all over him, laughing and carrying on. Kendra was the first to swing from the rope. She kicked her legs in the air and squealed, landing close to the bank on the other side. Sonnet didn't swim, but kept a good distance between us. I leaned against the tree and let a long, slow breath out, listening to the sounds of them playing in the river.

Biz and Lucy tried to climb on James's shoulders. He flung them off and flipped water in their faces. "Get you gone, you dwarfs, you beads, you acorns!" The girls laughed and doggie-paddled after him as he swam away.

"That's from Shakespeare," Sonnet said, her eyes trained on whatever she was doodling. "The dwarfs, beads, and acorn part. *Midsummer Night's Dream*. It's their favorite."

Sunlight flickered and danced and wove its way through the canopy of leaves. A tiny beam of yellow bounced off James's leg where he'd left it near me in the dirt. I leaned close to get a better look just as Biz scrambled up the bank. She wiped water out of her eyes.

"He wasn't born like that," she said. "It was amputated."

I sat up quickly. "Oh, I wasn't—I didn't mean to be nosy."

"It's okay, everyone wants to know. Well, everyone who isn't from here, because everyone here already knows. It was an accident."

"I'm sorry."

Biz shrugged. "He likes it because he got the prosthesis."

She said it slow, like I was too dumb to understand: p-r-o-s-t-h-e-s-i-s.

"I see."

"Johnny Austin bought it for him."

My heart fluttered two extra beats. "My Johnny Austin?"

She tipped her head to the side and looked at me with curiosity. "Sue and Kori couldn't afford one. Those are my moms. Sue and Kori, with an *i*. So Johnny Austin bought it for James."

"Oh," I said. "I'm happy he did that."

"We are, too. But now he's dead. I guess you know *that* at least."

She spun around and plunged back into the water. I was left alone except for Sonnet, whose pencil kept working the page.

Biz was right. At least I knew that much. But the question growing bigger in my mind was, just how much did I *not* know?

ELEVEN

The narrow aisles of the country store were as packed as a Georgia highway.

"Tourists," James said. "You can tell by what they buy." He nodded to a heavyset couple with a basket full of miniature, leaf-shaped bottles. "Vermont maple syrup is one of the biggest products for the tourist trade, but I guess you already know that."

Mama'd always made me practice my very best manners when we traveled, but these people seemed to have left theirs somewhere else. One lady pushed in front of another to riffle through bins of fresh vegetables, then she walked away complaining about the "lack of variety of summer squashes in Vermont." Three different people spun a rack of postcards at the same time, grumbling when one of them stopped the twirling to take out their selection. A bald man gathered a bunch of tiny blue and green flags in his hand and didn't leave even one behind for the little kid reaching for the same thing. The kid looked like he might perish if he went home empty-handed.

James reached on a high shelf for a new jar and let him pick one out. "Thanks," the kid said. "I really wanted one."

Even with all that rudeness, being crowded made me feel at home. I could hide in a mass of people like this. For a few minutes I relished the sense of being one of many, and not the center of attention, which, I was realizing, could be exhausting.

James maneuvered me toward the front of the store, where two women managed the customers together. One lady was stout with dark hair and muscled arms. She bagged items up and made suggestions on other purchases. Next to her, a tall, thin lady with a light ponytail punched the keys of an old-timey cash register. Every time she smiled, the corners of her eyes crinkled.

"That's Sue," James said, pointing to the short one. Sue looked over and blew him a kiss. "And that's Kori."

Biz climbed on a stool in between them. Kori automatically reached over to spin the seat so Biz swirled and giggled, her knees tucked up in front of her, her fingers curled around the edge.

"This is our second busiest time of year," James said. "Peak foliage season in the fall is first."

"What about in the winter—don't a lot of people ski here?"

"They do, but skiers only stop on their way to or from the resorts. Most of their time is spent on the slopes. They don't like to miss one minute of powder. Come on, I'll introduce you to the moms later when they aren't so busy."

We picked our ice cream from a long freezer. There were more flavors than I remembered seeing in any specialty store back in Atlanta, where ice cream is as important a part of summer as air-conditioning and swimming pools. James went behind the counter and wrote down what we took in a spiral notebook, then led us out the back door to a yard.

A barefoot girl twirled slowly in circles on a wooden swing hanging from a tree, flicking her toes at fallen acorns. Leaning against the side of an old barn, a boy about the same age sipped soda from a bottle and watched her spin. Every few seconds the girl looked up from under long bangs and blushed, pretending she hadn't noticed him studying her before.

"That's Haily and her new bf!" Lucy whispered. She had a dab of chocolate ice cream on the end of her nose. "It's her first one and the moms said we have to be re-special."

James wiped the ice cream off with his thumb. "Respectful, not re-special." He herded us to a picnic table on the side of the house. Lucy and Biz snuggled up on either side of me. Sonnet and Kendra sat next to James and watched me eat my Mexican chocolate ice cream cup as if I were the most curious thing to ever come to Vermont. No one had to tell me they weren't as keen about my being there as the two little girls.

Lucy nudged me. "Did you know it takes twelve pounds of milk to make one gallon of ice cream?"

"No, I did not know that. You're so smart."

"Lots of cows in Vermont," Biz said between licks of a cherry-chocolate-chip bar. "Ben and Jerry's gives their left-over ice cream to pig farmers, but the pigs don't like the Mint Chocolate Cookie flavor. Isn't that weird?"

"You girls are full of fun facts," James said.

A couple of fat, black-and-white speckled hens wandered near the table, pecking at the dirt.

"That's Harriet," Lucy said, pointing at the one closest to us. "And that's Georgia. Johnny Austin named her 'cuz that's where you lived."

"They're rescue chickens," Biz said. "Haily has to collect the eggs every day, but she doesn't like to. It's dirty. She wears dresses now. That's what happens when you get a bf."

"Sonnet can't eat eggs, she's allergic," Kendra said.

"Sometimes Harriet makes double-yolkers. You know what that means?" Biz asked.

"I can guess," I said, but my mind was swirling with thoughts of my daddy naming a chicken after the state where I lived.

I took a bite of ice cream and let my eyes wander around the backyard. Haily and the bf had moved out of sight. I wondered if they were hiding somewhere, kissing. One of the chickens strutted over to a grassy area where flowers grew around a circle of pretty white stones. In the center, a wooden cross was stuck into the ground. It tilted slightly to the left and leaned against a homemade sign that read "Here lies James's leg, kicking some butt in Amputee Heaven!"

They'd been telling the truth about the leg. My ice cream cup fell, but I couldn't look away from the little graveyard.

"Oh no, her ice cream! It's in the dirt!"

The chicken pushed through a clump of yellow daisies and pecked at something in the grass next to the cross.

"Pick it up, quick! Five-second rule!"

Kendra crawled under the table and inspected the inside of the dish. The cup was filled with dirt. "Sheesh, she wasted this one."

A leg, and even animals they had loved, were memorialized in that graveyard, right outside the back door for them to see every single day. And I'd never even thought to ask Mama where my own daddy was buried.

"Hey, what's wrong with you?"

"What's she staring at?"

"Maggie, you okay?"

I blinked really fast, aware of a quiet stirring going on inside my head. My chest had that melting-into-my-gut feeling, like I'd been walking on Mars for half my life, looking for a way to get home, and I was so close.

"Was he buried near here?" I asked.

"Who?" Lucy asked.

All the buoyant energy slowly sifted to the ground.

"The family plot is about twenty minutes away," James said quietly.

"Who?" Lucy said again.

Sonnet narrowed her eyes. "Haven't you ever been? He *was* your father, right?"

Was it my fault I'd never seen his grave? Mama should have taken me. Seems like no matter what else, he was responsible for my life. We should have gone as soon as we got here. I shook my head slowly.

"Do you want us to take you?" James asked.

"I'd like that."

TWELVE

James cleared the front seat of an old green pickup, throwing ropes and egg cartons and empty milk jugs into a box and putting it all in the back with Biz, Lucy, and Kendra. They sat up high on the wheel covers, Biz and Lucy on one side, Kendra on the other. Sonnet had disappeared.

"Is that legal in Vermont for them to sit back there?" I asked.

James adjusted the mirror. "To ride in the back of Mr. Green-Jeans? No, but in our town, no one cares."

He backed out of the steep driveway and we headed off down the road, his right foot working the gas and brake pedals, the sneaker on his left, fake foot resting on the floor. Traffic clogged up in the center of town. Masses of people crowded the sidewalks. A big family stopped in the middle of the road to take a picture without even caring that James had to slam on the brakes to keep from hitting them. I jerked forward.

"What are they doing?" I asked.

"Taking pictures, it looks like." James grinned at me. "Most of these are tourists and 4-H families. County fair starts tomorrow." He pointed to an overhead banner that spread from one side of the road to the other.

"I don't really know what a 4-H family is," I said.

"You've got a lot to learn about country living, then," he said.

We chugged through town and finally hit the open road. I sat back and stuck my arm out the window, letting the air make it rise and fall like a whip. The road snaked left and right, then straightened for a bit, rose up a hill, and dropped down so suddenly my belly tickled.

It was nice, driving in Vermont. Instead of concrete barricades and hundreds of cars zooming by, the side of the road was lined with leafy trees and stone walls winding their way through the countryside with us. It was miles before we saw another car. James raised his hand off the steering wheel to wave, and the lady coming toward us did the same.

"Who was that?"

He shrugged. "Just another person on the road."

I could see why someone might like to live here, if they didn't want a city life. Mama had to have a city. I thought again how it might be nice to come back and visit on vacations and drive on this road and sit on the front porch during the summers. After we went back to Georgia, of course.

Ten minutes outside town, we turned onto a gravel driveway between two stone pillars, drove slowly past rows of headstones, crested a small hill, then went down a slope. James eased the truck next to a tree with long, leafy branches. Heavy clusters of green acorns pulled the limbs down over a black iron fence surrounding a yard. A small, white stone house sat in the middle. The roof peaked over a leaf design with *Austin* embossed in the center.

"This is your family plot," he said. "Some of the headstones are so old the inscriptions are worn off."

I put my hand on the door handle. "Which one is his?"

James nodded toward the mausoleum. "He's in there."

"Is that place big enough for coffins?"

"No, only urns. He was cremated."

I tucked my hand back into my lap. The idea of going inside that building with jars full of dead people's ashes creeped me out more than thinking about going inside that barn the first day.

"Did you go inside at his funeral?"

"No. I wasn't there."

"You weren't? Why not?"

"Deacon was the only one," James said.

One of the girls knocked on the back window. "Can we get out?"

James looked in the mirror and put a finger to his lips.

"Your dad didn't want a funeral."

My chest squeezed tight. "That's why Mama said we didn't come, but part of me didn't believe her. She never liked talking about him much."

"She was telling the truth. We had our own family memorial for him, once Sonnet was ready."

"Ready for what?"

"She was with him at the accident. She was in shock, so we waited."

My brain swirled again. These people, this town, everyone knew so much more about my daddy than I'd ever thought to know.

"Mama said he got hit by a truck. Is that true?"

James nodded. "He was trying to open the door of a car that had gone off the road. There were people trapped inside. They said he slipped backward right when a truck was coming around a curve. Driver was texting. He went to jail."

"Where was Sonnet?"

"She was still in your dad's car. Luckily, she didn't see it happen."

"Was she close to him?"

"She was. They were a lot alike. He taught her to paint."

No wonder Sonnet looked at me like I shouldn't be here. I didn't want to get out anymore. I didn't like the way the whole thing made me feel. I wanted to go home and pretend

I'd never seen this graveyard. It had been easier in Georgia to not think about him; but here, in Vermont, my daddy was everywhere. I felt trapped.

"Can we go back now?"

"You don't want to get out? I'll go in with you, if you want."

"No, it's okay. Now that I know where it is, I'll bring Mama," I lied.

The truth was, I had no intention of ever bringing Mama. I wasn't even sure I'd come back myself. Sonnet had more right to him than I did. Now I understood why she hadn't come.

The girls pitched a fit when I had James drop me off at home instead of going back to their house. Biz and Lucy said they had something "really important" to show me. Kendra told them both to shut up.

"Don't say shut up!" Lucy wailed with tears in her eyes. James lifted her from the back and put her up front next to him.

"Sheesh, now I have to listen to them keep on carrying on about it," grumbled Kendra. "As if three months wasn't enough."

I had no idea what she meant, or what the girls needed to show me, but it didn't matter. I needed to be alone in my room for a while. I needed time and mental space to let everything I'd learned that day settle in my head. I needed time alone to think.

THIRTEEN

All afternoon my mind reeled. I couldn't stop thinking about graveyards and buried legs and Sonnet sitting in a car, waiting for my daddy to come back, not knowing he'd been killed, and me all the way down in Georgia, not knowing anything about him at all. At dinner I pushed food around on my plate.

"What's got you so sour tonight, little missy?" Mama said, stuffing a lump of tuna casserole in her mouth.

"What do you mean?"

"You've barely said a word since you got back from that boy's house. If I didn't know better, I'd think they brainwashed you."

"No one brainwashed me. I'm just tired. There are so many people in that family. I'm not used to all the noise."

She settled in her chair, satisfied, and nodded. "Well, there should be a law about how many kids a person can have, even the Catholics."

"Four of them are adopted, remember?"

"No, sugar, three. That dark-skinned girl is a foster—that's what the boy said."

"Hello, that makes you sound racist!"

"Excuse me, it does not. I'm simply identifying the one I'm talking about. And don't speak to me that way."

"Then don't call her that. Her name is Kendra."

"Okay, Kendra, then. She's a foster. I can't keep all the names straight, even that boy. He has the reddest hair I've ever seen. And that leg situation. I just don't know what to think about that. Did they tell you how that happened?"

"James. And, no, I don't know how it happened."

"Did you meet the mothers?"

"Just for a second."

She leaned across the table and lowered her voice. "What do they look like? I mean, can you tell?"

I stood up so fast my chair scraped loudly across the floor. "You really just said that? Was there something in particular you wanted me to look for?"

Mama's head flew back like I'd slapped her. Her eyes welled up, but I saw for only a second because she looked away quickly and started picking at her casserole.

"I'm sorry," she said quietly. "That was rude of me."

Mama's mood swings were as much a part of my life as one-hundred-degree summer days, but this sounded like a genuine apology. This was new. I didn't know what to say, so I sat down again and watched a hazy, red sun hover over the tops of the trees in the distance. Finally, she picked up both our plates and took them to the sink. I slipped away silently to my room.

After nine o'clock I was still sitting on my bed, reading *From the Mixed-up Files of Mrs. Basil E. Frankweiler* for the third time, when Mama knocked on my door.

"Come in."

She poked her head inside. "You didn't get dessert. Want some? Butterscotch pudding."

"No, I'm okay, thanks."

"If you change your mind, there's a cup of it in the fridge."

"Thanks."

"Okay, then," she said, hesitating. "Good night, sugar."

"Good night."

Her head disappeared and the door started to close. I jolted upright.

"Mama? Wait!"

Her head came back. "Yes?"

"Can I ask you a question?"

"Just one? That's not like you, but sure, shoot."

Big gulp. "You never told me why you and my daddy got a divorce."

Mama straightened up and crossed over to pull my curtains closed, like she had to think for a minute to remember.

"Why would you want to know that?"

"I was just wondering. I mean, I know we were here for a while, but I never knew why we didn't stay."

Something funny crossed her face, but she was still soft. "Let's put it this way: your daddy shouldn't have gone to fight in a war. It did something to his head. When he came home, he was different. He wanted to make it work, but he couldn't handle it."

"He couldn't handle me?"

"I didn't say that. He wanted us, but he was damaged."

"Damaged like sick?"

As fast as I could snap my fingers, the soft mood was gone. She shook her head and frowned. "I knew you couldn't do it," she said abruptly. "That's more than one question. Now forget about all this and go to sleep."

Before I could say anything else, she strode to the door and slipped out.

When the doorknob clicked shut, it was like a key opened a different room in my head. A room that had been waiting to be found for a long time. It was full of questions, and suddenly I needed answers.

FOURTEEN

Mama studied herself in the hall mirror and raised a mascara tool to her eye.

"Do you think I look old?"

She hardly ever asked me anything like that because she knew I'd give her a cheeky answer. It was like a game between us, and I almost always won. "Old as in an old cow, or old as in spoiled milk?"

"Okay, smarty-pants, don't get cocky. You're still young enough for a good old-fashioned spanking."

"You can get arrested for spanking kids nowadays."

She switched eyes and lathered black gunk over blond

lashes. "Well, they'd have to catch me first and now that I've got my zippy red Mustang, they'll have to up their game."

I raised my book in front of my face. "Whatever."

"In any case, I appreciate you waiting for the cable people," she said, sweet and tart at the same time. "It's been so long since I've been in a real, live city, and it turns out Burlington is less than two hours away! I practically have to drive that far to get to a decent grocery store."

"We've been without internet for three weeks now. I'm not budging until they come."

"Deacon will be home most of the day, but don't bother him unless it's an emergency. We don't want to owe him any favors."

"I don't need a babysitter."

"I know, but I might be gone until dinner. You'll be on the internet anyway. You can research all the trees you want and not have to set a foot outside. That must make you happy."

"Uh-huh. Twenty-first century and all."

She giggled and tucked the mascara thing into her makeup bag.

"Speaking of which," she went on. "Did you know there's a town in this state called Dummerston? You know, as in dumb? What kind of place has names like that? Only in Vermont, I'm telling you."

Her dig at Vermont irritated me. A month ago it wouldn't have mattered, but right then, it did. "Could be worse," I said. "There's one called Monkey's Eyebrow in Kentucky."

"Well, we can cross Kentucky off the list of possible places to move when we sell this godforsaken farm and get the heck out of Dodge. Or Dummerston, as the case may be."

I bolted upright so fast my book flew halfway across the room. "What do you mean? We're going back to Atlanta, remember? I emailed Irene before we moved and promised her!"

Mama looked at me through the mirror. "I make those kinds of decisions, and I am certain there isn't anything more for us in Atlanta than there is here in Vermont."

"What? No! What about my friends? My school?" Every layer of skin on my face was on fire.

She puckered her lips and painted them bright red. "I think you'll come to understand what it means to be so rich we can go anywhere we want."

"I don't want to be rich, I want to go home!"

She turned to me, tucked her purse under her arm, and said, "All things considered, can you honestly say where home is right now?"

I slammed myself down on the couch and turned my face so she couldn't see the tears stinging my eyes.

The cable lady showed up when I was getting the mail. I ran to the house, not sure which I was more excited about: finally getting internet or the pink envelope addressed to me from Irene. She was back from Europe. Finally! Communication from the great beyond.

On the front was a pastel watercolor of a pond. It was one of Irene's mother's cards. I'd seen a box of them on her desk the last time I was there. Her mother hand-wrote sympathy notes for people at her church, which meant Irene never had to be bothered actually finding a card when she needed one.

Inside, she'd written in curly script, "Miss you, ♥ Ireneeeee."

That was it.

That was all she wrote.

I checked the back. Nothing about our friends or her trip to Europe. Not one word asking how I was doing, one thousand two hundred miles away. My heart sank. I let the card drop to the floor and sat in the window seat, watching the birds by the feeders outside until the cable lady was finished.

"You won't be able to get cell service until your mother registers the unit with her phone company," she said. "But you've got internet and television today. Welcome to Vermont!"

As soon as she left I switched on all three TVs just to hear the noise, then pulled up my Facebook account and messaged Irene.

ME: Internet's up! Come chat!

Two hundred and thirty-seven notifications flashed on the top bar. One by one, I clicked through and deleted them.

IRENE: Hey!

Finally!

ME: Ireneeee!

IRENE: God, it's been like forEVER.

ME: I know, takes a bazillion years for the cable people to get out here.

IRENE: What's Vermont like?

What is Vermont like?

Outside the kitchen window, field grass swept across the landscape in gentle waves. A memory flashed of my daddy walking in that field, sweat soaking a gray T-shirt. I could almost hear his voice saying, *"Nothing like the sweet smell of fresh-cut grass."*

Was this a real memory?

IRENE: Yo! You there?

ME: Yeah, sry. It's okay, kind of weird, but it's pretty. Mama's different. She leaves me alone a lot more. She doesn't like it because we're so far from everything, but I don't want to be dragged all over Vermont just because she's depressed.

IRENE: Oh god, is she having migraines again?

Irene was convinced Mama's mood swings came from undiagnosed migraines. She was an expert Dr. Googler.

ME: Not too bad, not yet. How was Europe? Sry I wasn't there when you got back.

IRENE: Same as every year. OMG, guess what? Remember Randy, that new guy at the club with the blond hair that falls in his face like he's a secret spy and doesn't want anyone to see his eyes? Wanna know why he does that? Guess!

ME: He's a secret spy and doesn't want anyone to see his eyes?

IRENE: Okay, dork. No to the spy, but YES to the eye! He's

missing one entire eyeball!!!!!

ME: Only thing worse than losing an entire eyeball would be losing half of one. What does it look like?

IRENE: He has a glass eye. Just happened last year, so he's kind of shy about it, but guess what? I LIIIIIKE him!

ME: Just LIIIIIKE? That's not much, Ireneeee.

IRENE: LOL. He's coming over. We're going to the club to swim. I can't wait to see if he leaves the eye in.

ME: Be sure to keep me posted on that.

IRENE: What do you do up there? Is there a club? Have you started running yet?

ME: No, I'm not even registered for school. But I went swimming for the first time.

This was partially a lie, seeing as how I went with people who were swimming, but didn't actually swim myself. The truth would leave me open to Irene's questions and judgment, which could be plentiful. She was a little like Mama that way.

IRENE: Where? With who?

ME: A guy named James, he's in high school. We swam in a river across this field near my house—

IRENE: A river? Eewwwwww. That sounds gross. I don't even like it when they don't put enough chlorine in the pool at the club, but a river?

ME: I know, it creeped me out at first, but it was clean. I mean, it is Vermont. There isn't even pollution here. Not like Atlanta. And guess what, James has FIVE sisters! Isn't that cray-cray?

IRENE: Is he hot?

ME: No! I mean, he's old. I think he's going to be a senior. But he's just, he's James. He has super-red hair and he's missing a leg.

IRENE: Yuck. And he went swimming with you?

ME: He has a fake leg. It's not any grosser than a glass eyeball.

IRENE: Did he take it off when he went in?

ME: Duh.

IRENE: Shut up. What did you wear?

ME: My bathing suit.

Another lie. I was on a roll.

IRENE: Still the same one from last year? I thought we discussed this.

ME: I didn't get the new one yet.

IRENE: I can't believe that thing still fits. Wasn't it too small up top?

I looked down at my flat chest. Irene had always drawn a different kind of attention than me. She was one of those girls who blossomed early. For whatever reason, it made her feel good to point this out.

ME: No, not really.

IRENE: Wanna see my new bathing suit?

I rolled my eyes extra big.

ME: Sure.

A picture popped up. We used to laugh about kids who took selfies, but Irene had worked it to the max. Her hair was bundled on top of her head with little blond tendrils tumbling down around her ears. She had one hand on her waist, one hip stuck out, and her back arched. The bottom of her bikini was barely more than ribbons tied together.

ME: Do your parents know you're wearing that thing at the club?

IRENE: What's wrong with it?

ME: It's a little revealing.

IRENE: What, are you jealous? Worried your one-legged bf might like me better?

ME: A) He's not my boyfriend, and B) we are seven whole states away. If I had a boyfriend, you wouldn't be a threat.

IRENE: If you say so.

ME: I say so.

I could see she was typing, then pausing, then typing again. I fiddled with the pink envelope.

IRENE: I gotta go, Randy's coming soon. I have to shave my legs.

Shave her legs? Since when?

ME: Have fun.

IRENE: Yeah, bye.

ME: Bye.

I closed the laptop and watched the trees wave in a breeze out the window. It had only been five weeks since I'd seen her, but Irene had probably already moved on to a new group of friends. Maybe even girls with cleavage. I knew that last "bye" was for more than just our chat, but it didn't devastate me like I would have expected. In fact, it's possible I was a little relieved.

FIFTEEN

Back in Georgia, the thing I was known best for, other than being the only long-term friend Irene ever had, was my running. I wasn't curvy or clever with boys or pretty in a glamorous way. The only reason anyone knew my name was because the newspaper wrote an article about school sports and said I was the fastest sixth grader in all of Atlanta.

Rummaging through a box, I found my old running shorts, my field day T-shirt, and a fake bronze medal at the end of a loop of red, white, and blue ribbon. *High Point Field Day Champion*, it read. I dressed quickly for a run, then stuck my head through the loop and let the medallion hang against my chest. Hands on hips, legs spread apart, chin up, shoulders back, eyes strong, I took on the Wonder Woman pose. My coach made us do that every day before practice. She said it would give us the self-esteem of champions.

Outside, I took another deep breath and drew in the sweet scent of summer. Except for the blue cap overhead, and the occasional pastel flower that hadn't wilted, the whole earth had turned a thousand different shades of green. I followed the split-rail fence, jogging until I got to the far end of the field where a three-sided pony shed stood empty in the corner. Old, dried leaves had scattered across the dirt floor, and a few straggly pieces of hay clung to the bottom of a metal rack on the wall.

A breeze blew soft and cool on the back of my neck. I stretched my legs one at a time, then started off slowly into the woods, watching to place my feet carefully on solid ground. I was used to running on a level surface; it would be easy to twist an ankle here.

Remnants of a path spread between the trees. I ran along it, beneath scattered white birch and past dogwood laced with red berries in place of pink blooms. The deeper I moved into the woods, the more I felt a part of them, of the trees and earth and sky, and less like some girl transplanted from a city twelve hundred miles away.

The soil turned spongy under my feet. Every so often an area heavy with undergrowth gave way to a patch of sweet grass, soft like a baby's breath. Ribbons of light wound through the trees, touching everything in their way with a hint of gold. Finally, after running more than I had in almost a month, I gave in to aching lungs and stopped to gulp air that was fresh, damp, and comforting.

A woodpecker drilled holes, stopped, and drilled again. A chorus of birds sang their distinct songs. The only one I recognized was a wood thrush, and I knew that sound because it had been Peter's favorite on a songbird app he had on his phone. A stone wall started out of nowhere and disappeared past a place where the earth took a dive out of sight.

My heart still pounding, I followed the wall through the woods until it dwindled to a sad pile of rocks at the fringe of a glen where the path, too, disappeared. Trees with rough, gray bark grew far enough apart so the sunlight fell in waves instead of patches. The larger trees had metal pails hanging from their trunks.

Just ahead, an old, swayback building with two chimneys was almost hidden beneath tangled layers of vine and ivy. Barely visible along one side was a stretch of windowpanes crusted with layers of dirt. I pushed away heavy growth, snapped twigs underfoot, and trampled yellow-bloomed weeds to reach a door. Kicking away vines that had built up around the base, I pulled it open just wide enough to squeeze through.

The inside was one large room with a wall-to-wall fireplace that smelled faintly of old smoke and something sweet.

Wood plank shelving held an assortment of dusty glass bottles and jugs: blue and green and brown. Two massive cast-iron pots sat by the fireplace. I tapped one with my foot. A bevy of spiders scattered, disappearing between the wall and the floor. Light slanted through the crack in the door, highlighting particles of dust floating gently in the air.

The length of the room was taken up by a long wooden table, with a solitary, straight-backed chair sitting at an angle, as if someone had just gotten up and walked away. I sat down and ran my hand over the top of the table, as if maybe by feel I could know who had lived, or worked, here, and how long it might have been since the place had been useful.

Like on a Ouija board, my fingertips moved to grooves carved into the wood. I leaned close, trying to see in the dim light, and followed the pattern whittled into the corner with my fingers. A heart shape surrounded three sets of initials: JA + DA = MGA

Johnny Austin + Delilah Austin = Magnolia Grace Austin.

His voice was there again, all around me, so real I could almost hear it.

"We're going to carve our initials here, Magnolia Grace, so we'll be together forever, no matter what."

SIXTEEN

Deacon was pulling out of the driveway when he saw me coming up the hill an hour later. He stopped the truck and leaned out the window. "You okay?"

"Yeah," I said between gulps of air. "Just needed to run."

"Bet it's different running through those woods than on a track."

"Yeah, I had to be careful. Lots of rocks and stuff. How'd you know I ran track?"

He chuckled. "Your mama may not like me much, but she does like bragging on you. How far did you get?"

"Down to that old building."

"Ah."

I rested my hands on the open truck window. "What is that place?"

"It's the original sugar shack from your family's maple sugaring business."

"My family's what?"

"Maple sugaring. The Austins made syrup for generations. Didn't you know that?"

"No. I don't know much about them except they didn't smile when they had portraits done."

Deacon laughed and looked toward the house. Mama's car was still gone. "Got any place you have to be soon?"

"Nope."

"Climb in. I'll show you something."

I was covered head to toe with an assortment of woodsy things. Grass clung to my shoelaces, my ankles were coated with dirt, and I had already pulled a leaf from my hair.

"Don't you want me to shower before I get in your truck?"

"Quince and I don't mind—she'll move for you." He patted the seat and Quince obediently scooted close to Deacon.

"Okay."

We took a right out of the driveway and bounced and bumped and jostled along the road heading away from town.

"I think your truck needs some fixing," I said, holding tight to the dashboard.

"Suspension," he said. "I kinda like it this way. Only the strong survive."

I flattened my hand over the top of my head so it didn't smash into the roof. "I'm happy for you."

A stop sign jumped out from the thick bushes like a bull's-eye. We turned right and drove past trees on both sides that were so tall, and so lush, they almost met above the middle of the road. Ten bumpy minutes later, Deacon took another right onto an unmarked dirt road cutting straight through a jungle of trees. Deep ruts slowed us to a crawl until the road dead-ended in front of a long, gray building, as generous as any strip mall in Atlanta. I counted eight chimneys rising from the roof.

"What is this place?"

He shifted the truck into park. "This was what the Austin family's maple sugaring business turned into."

I rolled the window down with the crank handle and watched the forest beside me. Humidity seeped in, thick as fog, piggybacking the musty smell of wood and wildlife and greens. There were no pails attached to these trees, and no path to take me deep into the middle. Except for the opening where the building stood like a unwelcome guest, these woods had grown wild, carpeted with fallen limbs and skinny ferns nearly smothered by a knee-high quilt of last year's leaves.

"Why's it so far from the farm?"

Deacon rested his arms across the top of the steering wheel and looked out the front window. "You know how big four thousand acres is? Your father's family made maple syrup for over a hundred years. Started out in that little sugar shack you found today. In the early part of spring, there'd be buckets hanging from those trees full of sap. They'd dump it into big containers and haul them by horse and sleigh to the shack, then boil it down over a fire and make syrup. Your grandfather wanted to modernize, he wanted to make more money. He built this place up and installed miles of rubber tubing and shiny equipment so everything happened faster. He ran it that way for close to fifty years."

"Was my grandfather named Benjamin?"

"No, that was your great-grandfather. Benjamin never would have made it all into something like this. Your grandfather's name was Brandon."

"Why did this place get closed down?"

"Your father didn't like it, said the new processes made maple syrup taste like paper money. He loved the old place, and those woods. There's a poem that always makes me think of him, something about men being too gentle to live among wolves. Anyway, he wanted to paint and his parents wanted him to learn the business. He was miserable, so he left. Same story happens all the time. He didn't come back until after his parents died. You and your mama showed up not long after. When you left, first thing he did was shut this place down."

"What happened to the people who worked here?"

"He made sure we were all taken care of."

"You worked here?"

Deacon nodded. "Started in college, which I didn't finish

until your father closed this place down. He made it possible for me to go back and even get my master's degree."

"You have a master's degree?"

Deacon chuckled. "I may look a little rough around the edges, but, yes, I got my master's in counseling."

"I didn't mean to sound rude, I was just surprised."

"Don't worry, it still surprises me."

"I thought you worked at the store with Sue and Kori."

"I do, a few afternoons a week. More in the summer. The rest of the time I'm the guidance counselor at your school."

"Oh, wow," I said. Deacon would be at my school. That was comforting.

"It's a small town," he said. "Pretty soon you'll know who is who, and who works where and when, just like the rest of us."

"This man at the library knew all about my daddy. He called him a recluse."

"A lot of people called him that. But he was a good man. He did a lot for this community."

"Like donating the library?"

He nodded. "Like donating the library."

"I wish I could have known him."

"Well, that's why you're here now. So you'll know who he was before you decide what to do about the farm."

I turned my attention back to the old maple factory. I didn't feel comfortable telling him I already knew we were selling it. "What's this place used for now?"

"Nothing. A lot of businesspeople tried to buy it over the years, but your daddy wouldn't sell. Not until he knew whether you wanted it. Of course, he died before he could find out. So it sits."

It was late afternoon when Deacon let me off in front of the house. We'd gone home a roundabout way and stopped at his favorite hot dog stand. The smell of sauerkraut and mustard still clung to my shirt. I waited for his cottage door to close, then turned and let my feet take me back to those woods, back to the sugar shack in the maple grove my daddy had loved.

When I got there, the sun was sinking behind the trees. Dusky shadows replaced the golden light from earlier in the day when the sun was high. I moved from tree to tree and touched the metal buckets, lifting the lid on one to smell inside. Then I stood in the middle of that grove, closed my eyes, and inhaled sharply. It was easy to imagine wafts of smoke drifting from the chimneys of the sugar shack, gray and almost sticky with sweet. My feet felt rooted into the earth. I had come from this place. This is where I was always meant to be. Where I belonged.

Maybe Mama'd been right. Georgia was fading now. A new, exciting idea edged into my mind. A possibility. What would have to happen for us to be able to stay right here in Vermont?

The next day, another letter came for me, this time from Peter. Slipping my thumb under the edge, I tore the envelope open and pulled out a single piece of plain white paper folded into thirds. A check floated to the floor, but all I could look at was the painfully short note on the page it had been wrapped in.

Thank you for your letter. Good to hear all is well.

Peter

That was it. Just those twelve words and the check. It was like God, or the universe, was making sure I understood there wasn't anything left for us back in Georgia. Everything I needed was right here.

SEVENTEEN

A few days later James drove over in his truck with Biz and Lucy and an invitation to dinner. Mama answered the door and accepted on my behalf before even asking me. It was just as well; I was restless, and the image of poor little Lucy's crying face had stayed in my head ever since they'd dropped me off the other day. Besides, Mama'd already told me she was making clam chowder for us. I hate clam chowder.

The girls scrunched up next to me on the ride home. I was pretty sure that wasn't legal either, since we had to wrap one seat belt around the three of us, but I didn't ask. I kind of liked the way they adored me already.

"We have to meet you to the moms first," Lucy said.

"Introduce her," Biz corrected. "We have to introduce her."

"Okay, but then we're going to take you—"

Biz held her palm over Lucy's mouth. "Quiet! It's a surprise!"

"Oh good, I like surprises," I said.

"Girls, you're going to make Maggie want to run home as soon as we get there," James said. "They haven't stopped talking about you for days."

"I'm sure that thrilled Kendra and Sonnet."

"Don't pay attention to them," he said. "They're both a little on the self-centered side."

"Yeah," Biz said with authority.

"Yeah," Lucy mimicked.

Sue and Kori were stocking shelves in the store when we got there. Sue shook my hand so hard I thought the bones might break. "Happy to finally meet you, hon," she said before turning back to her work.

Kori hugged me gently. "You look so much like your dad," she said. "And that's a fine thing."

"Thank you, ma'am."

She waved her hands in the air and laughed. "Oh, no, that won't do. I know you're from the South, but you may not call me ma'am. That's my rule, okay? You'll make me feel old before my time."

"Yes, ma'am, of course. I mean, um, yes, Mrs. Parker, I mean—" My face must have been twelve shades of scarlet because Biz and Lucy couldn't stop giggling.

"Kori," she said. "Just plain, simple Kori."

The two girls each took a hand and pulled me toward the back of the store. "Come on, come on!"

Kori smiled again and waved good-bye. "Good luck, Maggs." My heart rose in my chest. She already had a nickname for me.

We went outside to where we'd eaten our ice cream a few days before, but we didn't stop until the girls had dragged me across the driveway, past the little graveyard, and all the way inside the old barn. James had a pitchfork in his hands. He thrust the tines into a giant pile of hay in the corner, then tossed dried grass over the side of a rough-built stall. Inside, a black and white pony buried its head in the hay and stamped black hooves at the flies. In the middle of its hindquarters, a black marking spread in half circles on either side of the tail, then trailed down to a point, making a near perfect heart. Biz and Lucy watched my face carefully.

"Is this your pony?" I asked.

They nodded.

"It's pretty. What's its name?"

"She's a mare. Her name is Sassy Pants," Biz said.

"I can see why you'd name her that."

"We didn't name her," Lucy said. "She came that way, but we didn't change it."

"I see."

Biz nudged past Lucy to get closer to me. "Do you like ponies?"

"I mean, I guess," I said. "I've never really been around them too much, but they're fine."

"If you got one, would you want to keep it?"

There was this group of horse-crazy girls I'd known since elementary school who cantered in the halls between classes and made whinnying noises when they met up with each other. They'd always been nice to me, even though I didn't ride, and invited me to their birthday parties. I didn't mind their behavior that much until they were still doing it in sixth grade and Irene made fun of them. When Irene picked on someone, she expected me to at least support her privately, but that time I couldn't. Not when those girls had accepted me in their circle even though I wasn't really one of them. It caused a big fight, but in the end, I hadn't given in and Irene lost interest in being mad.

"I wouldn't really know what to do with it," I said.

They turned to James at the same time. "See?" Lucy said.

"She doesn't want her anyway," Biz said. "I told you."

"I don't want who?"

James leaned his arms over the top board of the stall and stuck a piece of hay in his mouth. "They've been a mess ever since Deacon told them you were coming to live here because they thought you'd want the pony."

"Why would I want their pony?"

Sassy Pants turned around with a wad of hay sticking out both sides of her mouth. She took one look at me and laid her ears flat back against her neck. No one had to tell me what that meant. She felt as warm and fuzzy about me as Sonnet and Kendra did.

"Because she isn't really ours," said Biz.

Lucy shook her head from side to side, her little pink mouth turned down.

"Whose is she?"

Her voice was so tiny I thought I didn't hear her right. "Yours."

"Mine? How could she be mine?"

James pulled the hay from his mouth. "Johnny Austin bought her for you. He told the girls they could keep her here until you came back. They've been scared you were going to take her away."

"Why did he buy me a pony?"

"I guess because you're his daughter," James said.

"But I wasn't even here."

He shrugged. "Parents do weird things."

The whole thing unnerved me. The fact that my daddy bought a pony for me when I'd only seen him once since I was four years old was weird enough. But then, to give it to two little girls who were afraid she'd be snatched away someday—what was he thinking? Even if I had wanted her, I didn't know where we'd be after the year was up. What would happen to a pony if we moved away?

Sassy Pants stamped her hoof to dislodge another fly. She laid her ears back when she saw me looking, then shoved her face into the pile of hay. Biz and Lucy both looked like a flood of tears was about to burst from their eyes.

"I think you probably misunderstood," I said quietly. "I think she's supposed to be yours, forever."

EIGHTEEN

Kori told me that I shouldn't wait for an invitation to come over whenever I wanted. "Don't even knock," she said. *"Mi casa, su casa."*

"That's Spanish," Lucy said. "It means my house is your house."

Back in Georgia you never simply waltzed into someone else's house without being invited. Not even Irene's. This Vermont way of doing things took a bit of getting used to, but the third time Kendra had to trudge all the way down the stairs from above the store when I knocked on the back door, she made it clear my Georgia rules were a pain.

"Look," she said, "they like having you here, but I'm not the butler. Next time just come in, or you can stand out there until one of the parrots decides to get off the couch and come down themselves."

I wanted Kendra to like me because I was going into seventh grade, and she was going into eighth, which meant we'd be in the same school. She wasn't having any part of it.

On days I wasn't exploring the woods near the sugar shack or being dragged from town to town on shopping trips with Mama—who wasn't nearly as captivated by nature as I was—I spent my days putting books away as a volunteer at the library or I went to the Parkers'. There was always something entertaining to do there. Sometimes I did odd jobs in the store, like restocking the freezer with ice cream. Other times I walked to the far field to fill the water trough for Sassy Pants and the mule. I collected eggs in a wire basket whenever Haily forgot, and James taught me how to handle the pony without getting bitten so I could supervise Biz and Lucy, who had to have someone with them when they rode.

On a rainy morning in the first week of August, James called to ask if I would come play board games with Biz and Lucy. "The library needs me early, but I'm on babysitting duty. The girls already got into tussles with both Kendra and Sonnet, and Haily's not feeling well."

I laughed. "How could I say no to such a tempting offer?"

An afternoon managing two cooped-up girls was still more

appealing than staying home listening again to Mama's running commentary from the couch of her favorite villains on *General Hospital*. She complained about the daytime shows being stupid, but without anything resembling city life to occupy her 24/7, she was getting restless. The more restless she got, the more shows she added to her daily viewing schedule.

The Monopoly game was already set up when I got to the Parkers', and I'd been assigned banker. "We trust you. Not like Haily. She cheats," Biz said.

Lucy bounced on the couch, her tiny feet sinking deeper into the cushions with each jump. "Yeah, she cheats!" She had her hair pulled into two miniature pigtails, but it was so curly they sat on the top of her head like little gold balls. James glanced at me from the door and silently mouthed, *Good luck!*

An hour later, I was already losing when Kori came upstairs to make lunch.

"I got a house!" Lucy waved her arms in the air. "A house, a house, a house!"

Biz put her hands on top of the board. "Stop! You're gonna tip it over!"

Lucy bent down and placed her green house carefully on Atlantic Avenue. "I never had a house before!"

Kori kissed both girls and gave me a quick shoulder squeeze. "I wanted to convert the old garage into a padded playroom for days like today, but the pony won out, and now it's a barn. At least it means I get new furniture every year."

She disappeared into the kitchen. Pretty soon the whole house smelled of cheddar cheese and butter. "Grilled cheese sandwiches are ready!"

Kendra appeared from a hallway and walked briskly to the kitchen with her headphones on. Biz and Lucy abandoned me and Monopoly without even a backward glance. Sonnet slipped silently through the room, drawn by the same smell that was making my stomach growl. James hadn't said anything about lunch, so I sat on the couch, not sure whether I was supposed to go home now or wait for them to finish. I could hear them all in the kitchen.

"This one is burned on the crust. I don't want it," Lucy complained.

"Just pour ketchup over it," Kendra said. "Everything you eat looks like blood."

Biz giggled. "That's gross!"

"Yeah, gross!" said Lucy.

Sonnet passed the other way through the living room with a plate in her hands, her eyes on anything except me.

"Sonnet's leaving."

"Yeah. She's eating in her room again."

"Don't you worry about Sonnet—she's my business, not yours."

"It's been almost five months and she's still doing it."

"I said, it's none of your business."

Five months. It had been five months since my daddy died. Is that what they meant?

"Can't I have chocolate milk?"

"No chocolate."

"Why don't we ever get Kool-Aid?"

"Because then you'd be drinking *and* eating red, that's why."

"I don't put ketchup on my pancakes!"

"No, but you'd put red dye in the syrup if Kori'd let you."

"I would not!" Something slammed against the table. My stomach growled.

"Where's Maggie?"

Kori poked her head around the corner. "Hey, lunch is ready. Don't you like grilled cheese?"

"Oh, I didn't know if I was supposed to eat—"

Kori smiled and everything around her sparkled. "You silly, of course there's a sandwich for you. You're one of us."

One of us.

I swear I felt like I was walking on air all the way to the kitchen. Biz scooted over and shared half a chair with Lucy.

"Sit next to us, Maggie, right here."

"Yeah, sit next to them so they won't bug me," grumbled Kendra. She was already at the far end by herself.

"Be nice."

Kendra rolled her eyes and pretended to smile.

Kori wiped Lucy's face with a paper towel. "You and your ketchup face."

Haily burst into the kitchen, her hair all wild around her head and a red mark on her neck.

"Why didn't you call me for lunch?"

She grabbed a sandwich from a platter on the counter, plopped down at the table, and poured a glass of milk.

"I'm glad you decided to join us," Kori said. "I thought you might sleep until the next full moon." She walked over and pulled Haily's hair back, staring at the red mark.

Haily jerked away. "What are you doing?"

Kendra didn't even try to hide her grin. "Busted! You can't hide a hickey with hair. You need makeup, FYI."

Haily's hand went right to her neck. "What are you talking about? Shut up!"

"That's enough," Kori said sharply. "Come with me."

"I'm still eating," Haily said, stuffing the sandwich into her mouth and looking at her mother like, *See?*

"Put your sandwich down and come with me."

"I'm not done." She gulped two long chugs of milk.

"If you don't come with me right now, we will have this conversation in public, and I am pretty sure you would rather have privacy when we discuss the kinds of things that happen to girls who are loose with boys when they are only sixteen."

Haily glanced at me like it was my fault, then pushed her chair away and stormed from the room. Kori followed her. A minute later, Sonnet came in smiling.

"Could you hear?" Kendra asked.

Sonnet put her hand around her own throat and nodded.

"Ahhhh, she's gonna get it!" Lucy said.

Biz giggled. "So is the bf! Is Kori gonna tell his mom and dad?"

"I bet she does," Lucy said.

"Yeah," echoed Biz.

"She should know better than to waltz in here with that hickey sticking out like a smashed tomato," Kendra said.

Sonnet pointed to her own neck. "Yup, big hickey, big trouble."

"Yup, big hickey, big trouble," Lucy said.

She took a long drink of milk, then looked at us, her eyes all wide and blue, a white mustache dripping from her upper lip, and asked, "What's a hickey?"

Sonnet giggled first, then Kendra, then me and Biz, and pretty soon we couldn't stop laughing. Lucy's face turned crimson. I reached for her, thinking she was about to cry, but when she saw she was the center of attention, she grabbed ahold of her neck and danced around the kitchen on her tippy-toes, pretending to choke from laughter.

The sun came out after another game of Monopoly, and the girls begged me to stay while they rode Sassy Pants. Biz rode first, splattering mud around the paddock, while Lucy snuggled up next to me on the fence. She leaned her cheek against my bare arm.

"Maggie?"

"Hmmm?"

"I'm glad you're here."

"Me, too."

A half a minute went by.

"Maggie?"

"Hmmm?"

"Will you tell me what a hickey is?" she whispered.

I looked up at the brilliant blue Vermont sky, and the tops of emerald-green trees waving side to side, and smiled. It looked so much like the ceiling at the library. How many times had my daddy been here with these girls—the closest I'd ever have to real sisters—while they rode the pony he'd meant for me? How many times had he felt warm and loved by this family?

I put my arm around Lucy and squeezed. "Sure," I said. "We'll look it up together."

NINETEEN

Mama took me to register for school two weeks before Labor Day. She hauled along the biggest of my track trophies, a stack of report cards, and a copy of the newspaper article from the *Atlanta Journal-Constitution*.

"Trust me, sugar," she said, parking in front of a redbrick building in the center of town. "They'll put you on the track team without even a tryout when they see all this!"

"They've probably already started, and they may not even care, anyway."

"They'll care," she said, checking her hair in the mirror. "Let me do the talking."

It was hard to get excited about a new school year when I knew every day Mama'd be planning what she now referred to as "our escape." The more time we were in Vermont, the more I wanted to stay. I'd tried dropping hints, but either she was ignoring me, or she was completely immune to the possibility. Every few days she shoved new pictures of houses for sale in places like Houston and Los Angeles across the dinner table to me. She wanted to live in a place with "lights and traffic and lots and lots of noise." Looking at the photos made my stomach sour, but so far I had no plan to get her to reconsider selling the farm.

Mama gave the lady at the front desk our names. She was ushered into the registrar's office, and I was whisked off for a tour of the school with someone named Angela, who was wearing running shorts and a tank top. I followed her down a short hall and out a door.

"Our kindergarten through fourth grade kids are in this building," she said. "I teach spelling and grammar to the little guys, and English and social studies in the middle school, which is where you'll be."

"You teach at both schools?"

"We're all one school, just different buildings, and yes, we all cross teach."

"Wow, that's a lot of work." We walked over a grassy yard toward a narrow, two-story building.

"Not too bad. We only have a hundred and forty kids in all thirteen grades, so it's not that overwhelming."

"Wait, what?"

She laughed. "You'll find this is very different from a city school. There are only ten kids in your entire grade."

"Ten?"

"It's nice," she said. "Small town."

"Is there a track team? I was pretty good in Atlanta."

"We're very dedicated to our sports. And we know about your track history. Bob is excited to meet you. He's our track and field coach. And our basketball coach. And he teaches history to fifth through twelfth grades. You'll like him."

"Do I call him Bob? Or Mr. something?"

Angela grinned and pulled thick hair out of a ponytail, letting it billow down to her shoulders. "Bob will do. He's my husband."

"In Atlanta, if we didn't call the teachers ma'am or sir, we'd get sent to the principal's office."

"You might get sent down if you *do* call one of us ma'am or sir here," she said. "All of Vermont is like that, but you'll find our school to be even more liberal than most of the state."

"Don't say that to Mama," I said. "She calls it the *L* word."

Angela waved to a man loping across the grass with a large camera in his hands. "There's my hubby now."

Bob was every bit of six and a half feet tall, with dread-locks pulled into a ponytail well past his shoulders.

"Almost got the scarlet tanager," he said, pointing to a red dot in the sky. "Don't see them too often out in the open. That guy must be lost." He stuck his hand out and smiled, showing off teeth almost as white as Mama's. "Magnolia Grace, right?"

"She goes by Maggie," Angela said.

"Maggie," Bob said. "Nice to meet you."

"Thank you."

"Love that accent, girl. Mine's all gone now."

"Are you from Georgia?"

"Jamaica," he said. "Gudmawninimframtimahlandofdesunanwelcumtofiyuhcriss hom."

"Oh, stop showing off, you're making her blush," Angela said. "He's speaking Jamaican patois. Still slips back into it when he's mad or trying to impress someone."

"What did that mean?"

Bob's eyes scrunched when he smiled. "Good morning, I'm from the island of the sun, and welcome to your new home." He put his arm around Angela and squeezed. "And she's right, I was showing off."

"I wish I could make my accent go away. People look at me funny, or they try to pinch my cheek and tell me I'm adorable. It's embarrassing."

"Pinch them back," Angela said.

I liked these people already.

"Anyway," Bob said, "we already know about your track interest. What about academics—what are your favorite classes?"

"English and history were always easiest—I'm not a math girl."

"A girl after our own hearts," Angela said. "But I'll tell you, our math is taught in a very different way. You might end up liking it here."

I already liked it. Not the math, but the school and these people who were going to be my teachers and my coach—because of course I was going to do track. I liked the way the school buildings were laid out on a plot of grass that was greener than any pampered lawn I'd ever seen in Atlanta. Plus, it was right smack in the middle of town, across the road from a white church with a steeple pointing like a needle to the sky.

And once again I had that feeling that I was, and always had been, a part of this place, a part of the earth beneath my feet. Like déjà vu, only better.

Bob and Angela took me through the rest of the buildings. Behind the gymnasium, Bob pointed to a path leading into the woods. "Once we get outside in the spring, we run the trails first, then move over to the high school in Bell Township and use their track. The team is pretty competitive, especially in cross-country. I'm hoping someday we'll qualify for nationals. Maybe you'll help get us there."

"That's so cool," I said. "My best event was the fifty, but my favorite was cross-country."

"Atta girl! We'll have you all ready by spring sports season," Bob said. "I push my kids, but we have fun. Do you ski?"

"Water-ski?"

"Snow. I guess not in Georgia. One of the best things we

do to train for competition is cross-country skiing in the winter. We'll get you set up, you'll love it. Promise."

No one had to promise, I already knew I would love cross-country skiing as much as I loved to run. Maybe, if Mama saw I loved it here, that I fit in and was happy, maybe it would energize her enough to let us stay. Maybe she'd get involved herself, and get busy doing things that made her feel connected like I did. That's when I had the most brilliant idea ever.

"At my school in Georgia, we had a parent in charge of team uniforms," I said. "Do you have that here?"

Bob shook his head. "Not formally. The mom who used to do it moved on when her kid graduated and no one picked it up."

Angela crinkled her nose. "The uniforms are awful, gray with a burnt-orange stripe from the armpit to the hem. So last decade. Do you know someone who might want to take that on?"

Mama was coming toward us from the main building, waving her whole arm in the air and smiling like a kid who just won a goldfish at the fair.

"I just might."

TWENTY

Mama talked a mile a minute all the way home. The people in the office knew all about my daddy donating the library and painting that ceiling, and suddenly Mama was the most popular girl in town. This was the role she was meant to play. I bet since she was getting all that attention, she talked about my daddy like he was something special, and not her damaged and discarded husband from long ago. They'd even brought her a strawberry cupcake from someone's birthday lunch, which I now held wrapped in a napkin on my lap.

"We'll share it tonight, sugar."

When she paused to breathe, I dived in. "Remember how you hated the track uniforms at my old school?"

"Oh my God, those things were awful! I can't tell you how many times I tried to get them to change. For a school that costs so much money, you'd think they'd dedicate a snippet of that tuition to upgrade the uniforms, especially when their star runner got them written up in newspapers throughout the entire state! I am positive, without a doubt, that your team would have gone all the way to nationals if they'd let me get something with a little splash of color."

She waved one hand wildly in the air while she talked, and kept looking sideways.

"Mama, watch the road."

"You see how good you feel driving around in this bright-red Mustang? Just imagine how fast you could have run if you were in a uniform with bright, bold colors instead of beige and navy. Really! That's like eating plain vanilla ice cream when you've got a hundred flavors in front of you."

We pulled in the driveway. She jammed the car into park and flipped her head, looking at me over the tops of her sunglasses.

"You really need to wear a scarf when you ride in a convertible—your hair is flying everywhere. It's one thing to not agree to a touch of lipstick, but at least pull that mane of yours in a ponytail so you're presentable. Now, why were you reminding me about those god-awful uniforms? Oh no, don't tell me, are the uniforms here beige, too?"

I smiled inside. I had her.

"Worse," I said, like it was the most tragic thing that could have possibly happened.

"Worse than beige? What's worse than beige?"

"Bob and Angela said they've been trying to get a parent to volunteer to get new ones."

"What color are they?"

"Gray." I paused for effect. "With a thin burnt-orange stripe starting under the armpits."

The look on her face was priceless. "You have got to be kidding me."

I turned my mouth down at the corners and shook my head slowly.

"Are you doing track at that school?"

"If you'll let me, what with those awful uniforms and all."

Mama swung her door open and jumped out of the car, grabbing her purse and flinging the strap over her shoulder. "You can tell them they've got themselves a volunteer. I'll liven things up on that team, for sure!" Then she wagged her finger at me. "And one other thing, little missy, I don't care what they said for you to call them, we live by the Georgia rules, so to you they are ma'am and sir."

She spun around and marched away, shoulders back, head high. She got all the way to the front porch before stopping to say one last thing.

"And bring that trophy back inside. We've got to find a place to display those where there's room for more!"

I sank down in my seat, grinning so wide my cheeks hurt. The Stay-in-Vermont Action Plan just scored its first win.

My personal training program started the next day. Training for track, and training for Mama to see all the reasons we should stay. Every chance I got, I ran through the woods. I ran to the sugar shack and beyond. I ran through groves of trees with no path, breathing in clean, clear air without the oppressive Georgia humidity. I pushed myself harder every day.

I picked tiny purple wildflowers growing in places so thick with vines and foliage, almost no light came through. I touched every new tree I discovered, took pictures with my cell phone, and looked the trees up when I got home, then memorized the peculiarities of ash and beech, maple and elm. I ran as far as the back of the old factory, but I never went any closer than that. If my daddy hated it, I hated it, too.

As part of the Stay-in-Vermont Action Plan, I told Mama funny stories about Biz and Lucy so she'd feel like she knew them. Sometimes, I made the stories funnier than they really were. I'm not sure if she believed all of them, but she laughed, and she never told me to be quiet. That was a good sign. She knew all about Haily and the bf—not the hickey part—and the chicken named Georgia, and the grave where James's leg was buried, and how Kendra flapped her hand like a mouth when the little girls repeated each other. Slowly, Mama started to get interested in things around her. She joined a gym and went to Zumba classes, and asked me to take her picture so she could sign up on an online dating site. She was making it all so easy.

The first day of school, I got on the bus at the bottom of the driveway. Kori and Sue were driving Biz and Lucy, since it was Lucy's first day of kindergarten. James and Sonnet rode together in his truck, and Haily was getting picked up by the bf. Kendra was the only one who would be on the bus. I expected the same old silent treatment, but when I stepped up she was flailing her arm around from the back, trying to get my attention.

"I saved you a seat." She scooted close to the window and I sat down, baffled. "I'll show you around when we get there. We might even have a couple of classes together. Did you get your schedule yet?"

I shook my head. "No. Did you?"

"No, I have to get mine in the office. Yours should be there, too."

She looked out the window and the familiar distance crept in between us. Before the next stop, still facing away from me, she said quietly, "It's because I'm a foster."

"What is?"

"That I didn't get my schedule mailed. Everything has to go through the state. It's a big pain in the butt."

I didn't know what to say. I'd never known a foster kid before. "I'm sorry."

She glanced sideways at me. "It's not your fault."

As soon as we got to school, we ran into Sonnet standing in the middle of a group of girls. Kendra pulled me by the elbow and led me away. "Those are her art friends," she said. "They're totally cliquey."

"I thought you and Sonnet hung out together."

"We do at home. Not at school. I'm an outsider here. Just like you."

She turned into the office and left me standing alone in the hallway.

TWENTY-ONE

Autumn seized everything that was green, and turned the earth into vibrant oranges, yellows, and reds. The woods took on a different face. Everywhere was brilliance, every day a new experience. When I woke in the mornings, the air was brisk and chilly, but by midafternoon the temperature rose so my runs through the woods could still make me sweat. As soon as the sun started its decline, that warmth went with it. Frosty air nipped at my heels as I jogged the whole way home. Kori said it was called Indian summer. Kendra instantly objected.

"That name is derogatory to the Native Americans."

"There's no proof it has anything to do with them," James said. "It could have been referencing the country of India. No one knows for sure."

"Well, I know for sure," she grumbled.

With everything changing outside, my body was changing, too. Not in an Irene kind of way, but running tightened up muscles that had gotten soft over the summer. I could run longer without getting out of breath, and felt in control of my long limbs again. Angela noticed and stopped me one day in school.

"You must be training hard," she said. "I can see it. Only a couple of months before the snow flies. Bob will get you fixed up with skis and such in plenty of time."

I could not wait.

The last Tuesday of September, Biz and I were sitting on the fence behind the barn watching Lucy struggle with the pony. Sassy Pants had slammed on her brakes and thrown her head down to eat grass.

Biz put her face so close to mine I could smell her bubble-gum breath. "Saturday is Sue and Kori's anniversary!"

On the far side of the field, Lucy lurched forward and nearly toppled over the pony's neck. "Remember what James says, pull one rein," I yelled. "Make her head go to the side and kick."

Lucy grabbed the left rein with both hands and tugged and jerked and yanked and kicked with her heels, until finally Sassy's head came up and they trotted off again. Biz bounced on the fence rail, pretending to post to the trot.

"The moms want your mom to come to the party," Biz said. "I told them she looks like a movie star."

"What party?"

"It's a cookout. BYOCDS."

"BYOCDS?"

"Bring your own chair, drinks, and song. Sue plays the ukulele and Kori sings. You bring a song instead of a present and they play it for everyone."

"That's real nice, but I don't think—"

"Deacon's coming. He always comes. He brings his banjo."

It was nice that Mama didn't mind me spending so much time at the Parkers'; it was all part of the plan. But putting her into the mix was not. The Parkers were mine. Except for telling her stories, I wasn't willing to share them with her. Besides, hard as she might try, Mama could not warm up to Deacon. As long as he controlled her money, that wasn't going to change. If she came, I'd have to hear all her complaints about him for days after the party. That could easily be two steps back in progress. No, Mama would not hear about this shindig from me.

Lucy brought Sassy Pants back and jumped off. "Your turn," she said to Biz.

Biz climbed onto the first rail of the fence, stuffed her left foot into the stirrup, and swung her leg over the pony's back. Lucy handed her the helmet and Biz perched it on top of her head.

"I can't buckle this anymore." She held out the strap to

show me how it didn't fit under her chin.

"Her head got too big." Lucy giggled.

"You have to buckle it. Your moms said it was the rule."

"I can't. They know. It stays on, so it's okay. They ordered a new one for me on the internet."

Kori came around from the side of the barn. "Hi, Maggie! Thanks for helping the girls again."

"No problem."

I didn't tell her that the afternoons I spent supervising Biz and Lucy with the pony were often the highlight of my week. Without knowing if we'd be staying here, I'd taken my cue from Kendra and avoided making new friends at school.

Biz pulled the pony's right rein, kicked with both heels, and trotted away. "We can't go inside yet—I just got my turn!"

Lucy looped her arm through my elbow. "And I just got to be with Maggie, so I'm not coming either!"

Kori bent to pick up some red and orange leaves from the ground and smoothed out the lobes. "Look, Lu, these are a perfect color for your project."

"I'm still not coming, not until Maggie can come with us, and Biz is riding—we're not allowed to ride alone, so I'm staying out here."

"Manners, young lady," Kori said.

At the other end of the field, Biz pushed the pony into a canter. In three beats, they sailed alongside the fence. Biz's body swept up and down, up and down, with each stride. Over her head, branches dripped with yellow and orange leaves.

The smell of smoke from a neighbor's chimney mingled in the air. Lucy snuggled against my arm.

I'm happy here, I thought. *I belong.*

"—seemed a little confused about the song part," Kori was saying. "But she's game, so we'll see you on Saturday for sure!"

"I'm sorry?" I said. "Who was confused?"

Sassy Pants jerked to a halt and thrust her head into the grass again. Biz had broken a stick from a tree to use like a crop. She tapped Sassy gently with it on her rump and kicked.

"Your mom," Kori said. "The two of you can come on Saturday to the cookout. We roast a pig on a spit."

The back of my neck kinked. "You talked to her?"

Lucy bounced up and down on the fence rail, waving her arms at Biz. "Whack her harder! Whack her harder!"

"Earlier today. She came in the store to introduce herself."

"She did?"

Kori smiled. "Don't worry, Maggs, we're used to people who don't understand us. She was quite charming."

I had no doubt. Mama could charm the snakes off Stone Mountain if she wanted to. I also had no doubt whatever criticisms she could dig up about Kori and Sue and their lifestyle would be the topic of discussion for the next several dinners.

Biz yelled from the far end of the field. "Sassy!"

Kori and I turned at the same time. Biz smacked the pony's hindquarters with the stick so hard it broke in two.

123

Sassy bolted forward, Biz jerked back, and the helmet flew off her head. She toppled to the side and hit the dirt with her head and shoulder. Her left foot was trapped in the stirrup. Sassy snorted and spooked, trying to run away from Biz's body, which ricocheted off the ground, then landed with a thud, again and again as the pony galloped across the field.

Kori launched herself over the fence and ran, screaming, waving her arms, trying to block the pony. Sassy Pants spun around and flung Biz's body against the fence before taking off in the other direction.

Lucy screamed and clawed her way into my arms. Haily and Kendra ran from the other side of the barn. Haily's face drained of color. She pointed at me and yelled, "Go get Sue. Take Lucy and call nine one one. RUN!"

She and Kendra sprinted across the field to Kori, who was kneeling where Biz had finally landed on the ground. The pony panted wildly in a corner, her head high and eyes bulging. Biz's shoe dangled from the stirrup by her side.

TWENTY-TWO

S ue took one look at my face, one look at Lucy clinging
to me, and bolted out the back door. I punched 911 on
the phone and waited for someone to answer, then burst
into tears trying to explain what had happened.

"An ambulance is on the way, stay with me," the lady said.
"Stay on the phone until they get there—can you do that?"

"Yes." I was trying hard to stop crying because it was
making everything scarier for Lucy, but every time I thought
I'd gotten myself under control, I'd hiccup, then cry again.

"Is anyone else with you?"

"Her little sister, Lucy."

"How old is she?"

I pulled Lucy tighter to me with my free arm. "Five."

"Did she see it happen?"

"Yes."

"Okay, here's what I want you to say to her. Tell her, 'Help is on the way, it's going to be okay.' Can you do that?"

I jiggled Lucy. "Lu? The lady says help is on the way and it's going to be okay. Can you hear me?"

She nodded, her eyes still pressed into my neck. The back door crashed open and slammed against the wall. Sue grabbed the phone from me.

"This is Sue. Is the ambulance on the way?"

The 911 lady said something, then Sue said, "We're in the far end of the field on the left side of the driveway. She's not conscious."

Lucy wailed and gripped me tighter.

"Yes, I'm going now." She shoved the phone at me. "Put on the Closed sign and lock the door!" Then she disappeared out back.

Still cradling the phone on my shoulder, I hefted Lucy to the door, pulled the sign, and locked the bolt. The 911 lady was still talking. "The ambulance will be there within one minute now. Sit tight and stay on the phone. Let me know when you hear the sirens."

"It's me. Sue went out."

"I know, it's okay. Sue is a trained EMT—she knows what to do."

"I didn't know that."

"You must be new."

"Three months," I said.

"Got it. How old are you?"

"Almost thirteen."

"Well, you are doing the job of an adult and you're doing it very well. Be proud of yourself."

"Okay."

"Sometimes we don't get to pick when we start acting like an adult, do we?"

"No."

"I bet you can solve all kinds of adult problems already anyway, am I right?"

"I don't know."

"You should be able to hear the sirens now. Can you?"

I moved the phone away from my ear to listen. "Yes."

"Once you see them pull in, we'll hang up and you can get a book or something to read to Lucy. Keep her mind occupied. Do you understand that?"

"Yes."

The ambulance lights flashed red and yellow. The siren cut off when they stopped by the fence. "They're here."

"Okay, hon, you did a great job. Superb. You call me back if you need anything, okay?"

"Yes, ma'am, thank you."

"Good luck."

I hung up and wrapped both arms around Lucy. Through

the window I watched the EMTs brace Biz's neck and head and lift her onto the stretcher. Bile rose in my throat. The 911 operator had said I'd done the job of an adult. Right that second I think I'd rather have been able to bury my face in someone else's neck and still be the kid.

Lucy looked up when the ambulance sirens started again and yelped like a homesick puppy when she saw Sue's Jeep pulling out of the driveway right behind it. I smoothed the hair on her head, patted her back, and repeated words over and over like Mama did when I was little and upset. Somehow, in adult mode, those words felt useless.

Footsteps tapped on the stairs. Sonnet came from the back of the store, her face red and smushed like she'd napped through the entire event.

"Sue called. She said we should get ahold of James."

"Did she tell you what happened?"

She sounded like a robot. "Yes."

"It was horrible," Lucy sobbed. "She might be dead."

"She's not dead." I said. "They wouldn't have the sirens on if she was—"

Sonnet pulled an index card out of a box under the counter and handed it to me. "Call James. I'll go put the pony away." Her calmness was unnerving.

Miss Hilly answered on the second ring. "I have an emergency for James. May I speak to him please?"

"Is this Magnolia Grace?"

"Yes, ma'am."

"Haily already called. He's on his way to the hospital." She took in a deep breath on the other end of the phone. "I'm closing the library. I'll come get you and take you home. Just stay there with the girls for now, okay?"

"I can call my mother," I said quickly. I really badly did not want to have to ride even one mile in a car with Miss Hilly. She was always wound up so tight, and we needed calm.

"I'm already on my way," she said.

The phone went dead.

Thirty minutes later, we pulled up in front of the house in Miss Hilly's tiny Volkswagen. Mama rushed down the front steps, strands of hair pancaked between layers of tinfoil and artificial color. Her face was covered in red splotches and her eyes were wet.

"Oh my sweetness, my sugar. Deacon told me—he's gone to the hospital." She turned to Miss Hilly. "I was just getting something on my head to pick them up."

I didn't wait around to hear Miss Hilly give a breathless account of what happened. I'd seen the whole thing, live and in person.

Sonnet followed me and Lucy to the kitchen and went right to the fridge. "Do you have Coke?"

"Bottom shelf."

She pulled one out, found two glasses and filled them with ice, then poured soda into them.

"It's a Coke, Lu," she said, putting a glass on the table in front of us.

A few minutes later the front door banged shut. Mama

rushed into the kitchen and unattached Lucy's tiny arms from my neck, gathered her into her lap, and sat down, making cooing noises that sounded like the pigeons in Atlanta.

"Sugar, get us some rice pudding, would you? Rice pudding fixes everything—right, Lucy?"

Sonnet sketched birds in her notebook while I microwaved a bowl of pudding and tried to remember Mama ever holding me like that. One tiny spoonful at a time, she fed Lucy until her eyes got heavy, her head bobbed, and she finally fell asleep with her cheek pressed into a piece of tinfoil on Mama's shoulder.

"Can you pull this stuff off my head, please? My hair's going to be green after all this time."

I unwound the foil pieces and tossed them in the trash.

"Thank you. Now prop some pillows there on the couch. I'm going to try to lay her down for a bit," Mama whispered.

Even in her sleep, Lucy didn't want to let go and started to cry. Mama sank onto the cushions with Lucy curled into a ball on her lap.

"I'll just sit here with her, then. See to the other one, okay? What's her name again?"

"Sonnet."

"That's an interesting name. It must be Asian."

Sonnet scratched loudly in the notebook. I leaned really close to Mama and whispered, "It's a type of a poem."

"An Asian poem?"

"No, Mama. Just a poem."

* * *

James called about nine o'clock. Biz had been transported by helicopter to a hospital in Boston. He didn't have anything else to report, except to ask if Sonnet and Lucy could stay with us overnight. Lucy was already bundled up in Mama's bed eating ice cream with her. I gave Sonnet my room and curled up on the couch, since the guest room was still filled with moving boxes, but I couldn't sleep. I stared into the dark all night and wondered if I'd done something wrong to make the accident happen. Did Kori know Biz's helmet wasn't buckled? Should I have asked if the girls were telling the truth about it being okay?

I was still awake when the light outside turned from ebony to gray.

None of us went to school that day. Mama barely let go of Lucy for nearly twenty-four hours, except to let her sit on the kitchen counter while she baked tray after tray of biscuits, then fed them, slathered with honey and butter and Georgia-peach jam, to the girls. White flour drifted everywhere, including on Mama's eyelashes.

Around four o'clock, Deacon came to take the girls to Boston.

"Can I go with you?" I asked.

"Probably not," he said. "They'll be staying with family close to the hospital. Sue and Kori won't feel right until they're all together."

"Just on the drive there and back," I pleaded, stung by his

reference to their all being together when it didn't include me. "Lucy will feel better if I'm with her."

"Sugar, stop, let the family have privacy," Mama said.

She handed Lucy to Deacon, then wrapped up biscuits with ham and honey, and threw apples and a small Tupperware container of rice pudding into a bag and gave it to Sonnet. Lucy leaned over, grabbed the back of Mama's head, and kissed her on the cheek. Mama teared up, and put her palm over the place where Lucy kissed her, and smiled like she'd never been kissed by a child before. When everyone had left, I went into the bathroom and threw up.

TWENTY-THREE

There was no anniversary party on Saturday. No ukulele, no songs, no gathering of friends or pig on a spit. I was a nervous wreck all week, but Mama said I couldn't call to check on Biz because they were all probably too busy to talk to me. She didn't realize the Parkers were probably wondering why I hadn't called.

Deacon knocked on the door a little after eight on Saturday morning. Mama was still so hyper from the accident, she'd been up with the sun every day since. On this morning she was flying around the house in her nightgown, smearing peach-colored paint on one wall, sunshine yellow on another, and had targeted a third to test robin's-egg blue before getting my opinion.

"James called," Deacon said. "They're all staying with Kori's brother in Boston. They'll be there until, well, until Biz is better, or something. In the meantime, I'm going to try and run that store for them."

I leaped up from the couch. "I'll come help!"

Paint dripped from a brush in Mama's hand. "How is the little girl?"

"Brain injury. Still unconscious, but they're giving her something to keep her that way until the swelling goes down. She has a tube draining—" He pointed to the back of his head and winced.

"Will she, I mean is she—"

"They don't know yet," he said quickly.

"What about the pony that hurt that child? Will they get rid of it? It must be dangerous."

"What happened wasn't the pony's fault," Deacon said quietly.

I'd been scrambling around getting my shoes and other things I'd want for the day when I heard Mama say I couldn't go with Deacon.

"What?"

She dumped the brush into the bucket of paint. Speckles of blue flew out and landed on the floor, but Mama didn't even notice. "I want to help that family, sugar, God knows I do. But I can't let you anywhere near that pony."

"That's crazy! The pony isn't in the store—she lives in the barn."

"Maggie won't have to go near her," Deacon said. "Truthfully, I could use the help. It's peak tourist season. We need to keep the store open so the family can pay their bills."

She turned to me, narrowed her eyes, and wagged her finger in my face. "If I see you anywhere near that pony, I'll . . . I'll . . . I don't know what, but believe me, it won't be pretty!"

This was Mama's way of saying *I love you and I don't want you to get hurt*, without having to actually say the words. We weren't accustomed to doing that back in Georgia. But I wondered, if it had been Lucy, would she have been able to say it outright?

The store was a mess. Like a near disaster, unrecoverable mess, and it had only been open half a day since the accident. Vegetables had fallen out of the bins and rolled onto the floor, trash spilled from the can, sweaters and flannel shirts without hangers lay on top of the toilet paper shelf. Outside, people were lined up waiting for us to open. Deacon took a pot of coffee and a stack of green cups out for them to help themselves while we did a superfast cleanup.

From the second we let the customers in until the very end of the day, it was nonstop insanity. The tourists didn't know what had happened to Biz, so they didn't know how frazzled Deacon and I were just trying to keep up. They didn't know he'd never had a job where he used a cash register in his whole life, and that even though I was five foot eight inches tall, I wasn't a teenager yet and hadn't had any job, ever. They were not shy about pointing out the half-empty shelves. I couldn't run fast enough to keep them all happy.

At seven o'clock, Deacon locked the door and switched the sign to Closed. I collapsed onto the stool behind the counter and buried my face in my hands.

"I'm sorry. I'm so sorry."

"It's okay," he mumbled every time I wailed. "We did our best. That's all we can do."

In my head, I knew none of the craziness in the store that day was my fault. I also knew I wasn't responsible for Biz's accident, and I'd done the best job I could in both things. But in my heart, I felt like a big, fat failure.

Deacon drove me home and came inside to tell Mama why I was so overwrought. "I don't know how I would have made it today without her," he said.

A hot bubble bath never felt so good as the one I got that night. I scrubbed and scrubbed my whole body, as if I could wash away the voices of those customers complaining in my ear. I climbed into bed, still wrapped in my towel, and fell asleep. It was the first time I slept through the night since Tuesday.

Mama didn't want me to go back the next day. I knew Deacon wasn't expecting me, but I couldn't leave it all to him. I just couldn't, especially after saying he wouldn't have made it without me on Saturday. Besides, if I couldn't be with the Parkers, it was one thing I could do to still feel like I was a part of them. One little thing they'd appreciate when they got home.

You're one of us.

But I wasn't, not really. If I had been one of them, I'd be in Boston, not at home with Mama, who apparently liked Lucy better than she did me anyway.

Early in the morning, I grabbed my jacket, left Mama a note on the kitchen table, and walked to the store. As soon as she got up and realized where I was, she'd make me come home, but at least I could help Deacon get the day started until then.

He was restocking the jam aisle when I came through the back door. "Does your mama know you're here?"

I hung my jacket on a hook. "She'll find out as soon as she gets up. I left her a note. What needs to be done first?"

He paused, two jars of blueberry preserves in his hands. "You sure?"

"I'm sure."

"Okay, the clothing section is a mess again. Why don't you start there, I'll finish this, then we'll reevaluate."

"I'm on it."

The store didn't open until eleven, seeing how it was Sunday. By the time Deacon unlocked and flipped the sign to Open, we had it in pretty decent shape. Not like if Sue and Kori were running it, but good enough. Tourists poured in so swiftly it didn't take long to get behind again. Deacon punched keys on the cash register and checked people out as fast as he could. I did my best to answer the nonstop flow of questions, while running back and forth to keep the shelves full.

"Young lady, young lady!"

"Yes, ma'am?"

A woman pointed to an empty section. "Don't you have the big tin cans of maple syrup?"

"One second, I'll get it for you."

When deliveries came, Sue made sure the boxes in the storage room were stacked so the labels faced out. ("That way if someone needs to find something quickly, it's printed right on the front.") I said a silent thank you and ran to get the large syrup. But the lady didn't want a can quite that big.

"Do you have one that's a little smaller? In-between size. I can't carry that on a plane."

I made the trip again and brought her the in-between size.

"How much is it? There's no price."

"I'm not sure. Deacon will know up front."

She looked at me like I was the biggest idiot in the world and said, "Don't you work here?" then walked away without even a thank you. I wanted to throw something at her back and shout that I was only twelve, but three other people were waiting for me. Instead, I plastered a smile on my face and went to help them.

"Do you have that white fudge without nuts? Last year

you had it. I can't eat nuts, but the white kind is my favorite."

"Is this butternut squash? Or acorn?"

"Your apples are bruised. Do you have any fresh ones in the back?"

"What's the date on the cider?"

"Do you have Ben and Jerry's? You can't come to Vermont without getting Ben and Jerry's."

"I like this sweater, but I want one in blue, do you have blue? Sky blue, not dark."

Up front, Deacon had run out of bags. "Maggie, bags! Can you get them?"

Bags. Bags. Bags. My mind went blank. A lady at the counter watched me, tapping her feet.

"Where's that girl? We need help over here."

"Don't you have Sorel boots? We want the fuzzy kind, like what's in the ad."

"Maggie! Bags, please!"

Now he was shouting. The lady reached across the counter to get her money back. A bus pulled up out front and let loose a mass of new tourists. They swarmed and spread out through the store like a SWAT team. I looked at the clock. It wasn't even noon yet.

I ran to the back for extra bags. Bags, bags, bags. Looked in the closet, at the labels on the boxes, even in the laundry room. Where the heck were the bags? I ran to the counter. The lady had left, but there was a long line waiting to be checked out and Deacon was sweating.

"Did you get the bags?"

"I can't find them."

"They're in the back, in the closet."

"I looked, they aren't there."

"Damn," he said under his breath. He went to check for himself, and came back with a box of lilac-scented trash can bags. "This will have to do for now."

"Is there someone who can help me back here? I've been waiting."

The bell on the door binged. Just when I thought the top of my head might explode, and the tension in the store vibrated like an electric wire, Mama strode in, all dressed up like she was going to church.

TWENTY-FOUR

The way she looked me up and down with her mouth set in a straight line made my stomach plunge to my toes. She spun around to face Deacon, gripping her fancy purse to her side. Her back was rigid. I shouldn't have come. I should have woken her up or been extra nice in the note. I should have done something I didn't and now we were all going to pay.

Deacon looked at her meekly and shrugged. "Bags? We can't find the bags."

"Young lady, did you hear me? I've been waiting!"

Mama swung around when she heard the man talk to me

that way and marched toward him, her fist clenched like she was about to belt him a good one in the mouth. I couldn't make my feet move to stop her. It was like they'd been super-glued to the floor.

The look on her face must have scared him off because he ducked around a corner before she got halfway there. She didn't follow him, though. She stopped and bent down in front of the aspirin shelf, opened a drawer underneath, and pulled out a stack of brown paper bags. Then she stalked back to the front of the store and slapped them on the counter in front of Deacon.

"I just happened to be here last week when they decided to move the bags and make room for more syrup in the back," she said. Then she threw her tiny purse on the stool and turned to face the crowd of people who were waiting to be checked out.

"Hi, y'all," she said, real loud. "Welcome to our store. I'm so glad you stopped by. I know you're wondering what a pretty girl like me with a southern accent is doing way up here in Vermont running this country store when I could be travel-ing the world—am I right?"

She grabbed a green cup from behind the counter and filled it with fresh coffee.

"Here you go, hon," she said, handing it to a lady in line. "Do you like cream? Sugar? Just black? Okay, then, enjoy. It's on the house."

Customers who'd been crowding the far aisles came up

with their baskets full of trinkets and treasures when they heard the lady with the super-southern accent talking.

"I'll tell you why I decided this was my life's calling," she said. "It's because of you"—she pointed to a man who'd been grumbling about the size of tomatoes—"and you"—she nodded at a lady who had literally stamped her foot not three minutes before when I wasn't fast enough to help her—"and you, you sweet little thang." She handed a fussy toddler a toy from the shelf.

Then she flipped open a brown bag and started throwing a customer's items in it, all the while telling the most amazing stories about how she'd traveled the world, looking for just the right place to settle down and raise her daughter— this is when she pointed at me. She went on and on, spinning the most incredible tales about visiting the Taj Mahal and Buckingham Palace—she called it BuckingTON Palace, but I don't think anyone caught it—while Deacon smiled to himself and kept punching keys on the register.

If I didn't know she was my own mama, I'd be mesmerized, too. She was beautiful and young and dressed up all fancy like she just stepped out of a fashion magazine, and she was working that accent like nobody's business. She made every person in that store feel like they were the most important customer of the day. Everyone was greeted with a giant "Howdy!" or "Hi, y'all!" and she just kept right on talking.

One woman, who came in for toothpaste, left with a new

red sweater because Mama told her it would go perfect with her green eyes. I don't know how she even knew they were green because the woman had those odd, old-lady eyelids that sucked in the lashes and dropped down over her eyeballs. Mama even made up some story about the person who hand knit that sweater and most of the clothes in the store.

"Well, except for the nighties, of course, those are flannel, because it gets so chilly up here in Vermont at night. We locals all wear flannel." She crossed her arms over her chest and pretended to shiver. "Brrrr." Two women left the line and came back with nightgowns with moose and bears all over them.

"You know, those are exactly the ones I would have picked out for you. And I went to fashion design school in college, so I know what looks right."

The ladies blushed, paid for their purchases, and walked out smiling.

Mama kept up her shenanigans for two solid hours without so much as stopping to catch her breath. One by one, I helped customers while she worked her magic on the others and bagged items for Deacon in between. I'd never seen her do so many things at one time in my life.

At two o'clock there was a lull in the store for ten whole minutes. When the last customer walked out, Deacon plunked down on the stool and started laughing so hard his shoulders shook. When he could talk again, he looked at Mama and said, "Well, well, Delilah, who would have thought? You are something else."

Mama acted all fake surprised, like she had no idea what he was talking about, then put a hand on her hip and smiled smugly. "And don't you ever forget it, either."

I stood in the middle of the candy and syrup aisle and finally let loose the flood of tears that had been building up since we'd opened the store.

"What's wrong with you, sugar?"

"Those people were all so mad before you got here. It was awful, they were so mean, and then they were so nice. How did you do it?"

"Well, shoot, the same way I always get through the tough times, sugar. I faked it."

Mama pulled stuff together and made sandwiches for me and Deacon. While we scarfed them down, she got out the dustpan and broom and cleaned up so when customers started trickling back in, the place had less of a hurricane look.

"I'm going to the big grocery store," she said, tucking a loose strand of hair behind my ear. "You both deserve a nice home-cooked meal after this."

She was halfway out the door when she stopped and called over her shoulder, "That means you, too, Deacon. Dinner's at seven."

We closed the store at four o'clock, which was an hour early even for a Sunday. Deacon said we'd earned our keep. "You did well, Maggie. You really stepped up to the plate."

"I don't feel as much of a failure like I did yesterday, but that's mostly because of Mama."

He laughed. "That was something to see, wasn't it?"

"Yeah. It was kind of crazy, but she helped us out, right?"

"She sure did. It will be a great story to tell Kori and Sue when they get home."

"Yeah."

The reminder that the family was gone made me think of Biz, lying unconscious in a hospital bed. Boston felt very far away.

"Is there anything else I should do to help Biz?"

Deacon shifted his truck into drive and pulled down the driveway. "Wouldn't hurt to pray."

"Like in a church?"

"You can pray anywhere."

"I'm not sure how."

"Just start talking. God hears everything."

"What if I mess it up?"

"No such thing. And remember, Biz is still with us. Where there's life, there's hope."

I liked the way that sounded. *Where there's life, there's hope.*

He dropped me off by the front porch. My feet landed on the soft grass, and my legs quivered like they used to when I'd line up at the start of a race. As exhausted as I was from two days in that store, I needed to run. I needed to inhale the musky scent of fallen leaves that lay brown and moist under my feet. I needed to be where my legs rose from the soil, where my daddy had carved our initials into a table so we'd be together forever. I needed to be at the one place that always felt the same.

I took off down the field toward the birch trees, inhaling air that held the sweet smell of apples and decaying earth. Late-day sun pushed through red and orange foliage, dappling the gray stone wall in a pinwheel of color, but I didn't stop to look. I couldn't stop until I got all the way to the sugar shack and dropped into the chair, out of breath, and lay my cheek over the heart in the wood.

Closing my eyes against salty tears, I listened to the silence for a moment, then whispered, "Dear God—"

TWENTY-FIVE

O n Monday, Mama said if I could help run a store like I
did over the weekend, I could sure get myself back to
school. It was my first time being there without any
of the Parker kids around and I felt like I was missing my
left arm. Even Deacon's office door was closed tight. I was
on my own.

At lunch I sat on the steps outside with my paper sack
in my lap. Two of Sonnet's art friends watched me from the
little-kid playground. The tall one said something to the
short one, and they walked toward me together.

"It's Maggie, right?" the tall one asked.

"Yes."

"I'm Aspen. This is Jane. We're friends with Sonnet."

Jane had a purple streak in otherwise white hair.

"Hi," I said.

"Sonnet texted us. She said you were really brave," Jane said.

"Sonnet said that?"

They both nodded.

"We knew your dad."

Everybody knew him, I thought. *Everybody but me.*

Aspen held up her lunch bag. "Can we sit with you?"

"Sure."

Did that mean I should move over so they could sit next to each other? Or make them sandwich me? Sandwich it was. Aspen sat on my left, Jane on my right. They pulled food out of their bags and talked as if we ate together every day.

"What did you bring?" Jane asked.

Aspen passed a tiny jar filled with some kind of crunchy stuff to Jane, who took it and sniffed.

"God, isn't that what you had yesterday? And the day before?"

"Yeah. Mom's so proud of herself for making granola I'll probably have to eat it every day for a year. Man, what I'd do for a Girl Scout cookie." She picked through the jar, pulling out dried berries and almonds.

Jane unwrapped a stack of cucumber circles and carrot sticks, and stuck her nose near a tiny plastic tub of hummus. "Yuck."

I pulled out a plastic ziplock bag stuffed with Thin Mints

and Savannah Smiles. Aspen and Jane's eyes grew big.

"You guys can have them."

"Are you sure?" That was Jane.

Aspen grabbed the bag. "Of course she's sure—didn't you hear her?"

"Wow, thanks. This is awesome. Your mom gave you these?"

"I make my own lunch."

"Lucky."

They split the cookies up and chewed happily while I ate my half peanut butter and honey sandwich. Jane licked Savannah Smiles powder from her fingers.

"You're cool."

"Yeah," said Aspen.

This was how Biz and Lucy might be when they were teenagers, I thought. My stomach twisted. Would Biz even get to high school? There'd been no word since Saturday.

"We got to go with Sonnet to your dad's house once," Jane said.

"Because we're art students, in case you were wondering why."

"Oh, yeah."

Aspen leaned in and lowered her voice. "He let us see the magnolias."

They watched me like a dog waiting for a ball to be thrown. I smiled and stuffed the leftover crust of my sandwich inside the bag.

Jane looked at me suspiciously. "Your name is Magnolia Grace, right? They're you?"

The only thing I could do was nod. I had nothing else. My name was Magnolia Grace, but whether "they" were me or not I couldn't say, since I didn't know what "they" were.

"He hardly let anybody see them, you know, but since we're friends with Sonnet, and he and Sonnet were like this . . ." She crossed her middle finger over her forefinger and held it up in front of my face.

"Right," I said.

Yes, I knew my daddy and Sonnet were "like this." I knew she was there when he died and that whole family, who were now together in Boston without me, grieved for him when I couldn't. I knew he painted the ceiling of the library he donated, and some man had called him an ahh-tist. I knew Jeffrey said he didn't get out much, and Deacon said he loved the woods and the old sugar shack. I also knew that these girls, like everyone else in the universe, knew more about my own daddy than I ever would.

I got up without saying anything and walked away.

TWENTY-SIX

By the time I got home that afternoon, my feathers were ruffled enough that I decided to confront Mama. I deserved to know more about my own daddy. I'd been respectful of her needs the whole time we lived in Georgia and hadn't pushed when she shushed my questions. Now we were in Vermont. The rules were different. But she wasn't home. Neither was Deacon. He was at the store and I was agitated enough that I didn't want to go help him. I wanted to help myself.

I threw my backpack on the porch, crossed the yard, went inside the barn, and climbed the stairs to the second floor.

Two big doors in front of the landing had been pinned open ever since I got to Vermont. Deacon said the loft was used to store hay, back when the farm had working horses. They had cut it in the fields, then used a pulley to haul each bale up through the opening, and fed it to the horses all winter.

Outside those doors, blue sky pushed gray-ridged clouds swiftly away. Past the trees lining our road, blocks of wheat-colored fields—bordered by crimson, orange, and green—made the earth look like a patchwork quilt. In the distance, two red silos dotted the view, and even farther out I could see the blue sliver of a lake.

I could have stayed right there and looked at that view until the sun set, but I was on a mission. I hadn't seen my ancestor portraits since the day Deacon and I carried them out of the house, and I wanted to sit with them. They belonged to me. Not just the portraits, but the people. They were all I had left of my real family. No matter how close I ever got to the Parkers, I'd never really be one of them.

Partway around the walkway was a door that opened to a dark room. I reached in and flipped the light switch on the wall. Boxes with *Austin Ancestor Portraits* written in black marker sat in the middle of the floor. They were taped shut across the top.

More boxes, the same shape and size, were stacked in rows behind them. The tape across the first one had peeled off and fallen to one side. I carefully stripped it away, reached into a thousand pink Styrofoam peanuts, and lifted out a framed landscape with his signature across the bottom. *Johnny Austin.*

Styrofoam flew everywhere. Little balls stuck to my jeans, blew across the floor, and clung to the canvas. I carried the landscape to the light in front of the open doors and held it up. It was exactly the same as the scene outside. He'd painted the view from the second floor of that barn—the rolling hills, the two silos, even the strip of blue water in the distance.

I don't know much about art, but I could tell his was different. Something about the colors not being too bright, and the way light shone so everything on one side looked soft. Not in a Hallmark card kind of way, in a real way, like an invitation to step inside the scene. I turned it over. On the back it said *The Georgia View.*

All the other boxes were taped up tight, and labeled on the side like this:

JA/Vermont Draft Horses and Sleigh;

JA/Flooded Covered Bridge;

JA/Birches;

JA/Sugaring Done the Old Way.

No mention of a magnolia. Not one. What were Aspen and Jane talking about?

I shoved the boxes back in place, chased Styrofoam peanuts across the floor, and went in search of a trash can to hide them. Technically, everything in this barn was mine. I should be allowed up here, but it felt like snooping. No need for a piece of Styrofoam to give me away.

In the corner, an olive-green tarp lay over something that could have been a trash bin. I lifted the corner and peeked, hoping it wasn't home to a bunch of bats or something equally creepy. Underneath the tarp was a wooden crate, sectioned inside by slats of wood that protected a series of unframed canvases. Carefully, I pulled one out and leaned it against the wall. My breath caught. This was nothing like the land-scapes. This canvas was painted in deep shades of navy and plum, chocolate, evergreen, and a smoky pink. The dense background was broken up only by the image of a small girl in a white dress running beneath a tree that had thick, shiny leaves on branches loaded with cups of creamy magnolia blooms.

There were seven canvases total. They were all almost the same: a magnolia tree, a dark background, and a girl who looked slightly older with each one. The last one was unfin-ished, with smudges of the dark colors and a few magnolia blooms at the top. Underneath the flowers was the outline of a tall, faceless girl running with her arms stretched out and palms up.

Purple lights darted past my eyes. I put a hand to the wall to steady myself, and his voice was there again.

"I'm going to paint you, Magnolia Grace," he'd said. "One portrait every year." I hadn't wanted to stay still for him, so he'd moved his canvas and paints and brushes outside next to the barn where I could run around and play in the grass while he tried to capture my image. He'd made me laugh so hard I

ended up with a tummy ache. Later, he'd rocked me to sleep, my cheek pressed firmly against his sweat-stained T-shirt, the sound of his heart beating in my ear.

With shaky hands, I carefully placed each canvas back into its slot, covered the crate with the tarp, and slipped out the door. Sprinting across the yard, I grabbed my backpack from the porch, bolted upstairs, and locked myself in my bedroom. The photo of me and my daddy on the carousel was still tucked inside my copy of *Charlotte's Web*, where it had lived for over six years. I held it by one corner and lay flat on my back, studying the image. The need to confront Mama was gone. Everything I wanted to know at that moment, I'd seen in the magnolia paintings. And for the first time I could ever remember, I missed him.

TWENTY-SEVEN

The most amazing thing happened over the next three weeks. With the Parker family still in Boston, people from all over came to help at the store. Deacon said he could identify folks from at least five different counties spread from one side of the state to the other. I said there were a whole lot of people who loved the Parkers, but no one missed them more than me.

I learned what 4-H was when the kids showed up every afternoon to take care of the animals, and I got to know the track team really well when Bob had me teach them how to stock shelves. Angela gave her students extra credit for doing chores like hauling trash to the dump, and one of them wrote an article about community spirit for the newspaper.

Bob gathered a bunch of us kids together one day and took a photo to go with the article. It was printed right in the middle of the front page in black and white. There were eight of us standing with linked arms and smiling faces under the painted sign that read Parkers' Country Store. I cut the photo out and taped it to the fridge where Mama'd have to see it every time she opened the door.

People from the church with the steeple came to help customers. Deacon told me in secret that none of them were as much fun as Mama. One lady was a retired bank teller. She sorted out receipts every night, marked things in a book, and deposited money the next day. Then, a cross-country truck driver named Harold, a regular customer who came every other week to pick up fudge for his wife, delivered suitcases full of clean clothes and homework assignments to the family in Boston. Even Haily's bf, who turned out to be called Ethan Edward, kept the yards in front and back of the store raked. I'd never seen anything like it.

"It's called camaraderie," Deacon said. "Look it up."

On the days Deacon didn't need me after school, I ran. Running wiped the clutter out of my head and helped me think. I had a lot to think about. Finding the magnolia paintings had magnified my connection to my daddy to the zillionth degree. It was like reading his personal diary, and every word was an expression of how much he missed me.

After a few days, I stopped going up to look at them because every time I did, I left feeling sad about the years I wasn't here, and anxious about how desperately I wanted Mama to let us stay.

On the day Biz was moved out of the ICU, Deacon went to a florist the next town over and bought a bunch of shiny red, green, and blue balloons and tied them to a tree by the road. Everyone who came in that day got a cup of sparkling cider. Ethan Edward connected with Haily on FaceTime, and after they acted all secret and mushy for a few minutes, Haily passed the phone around so we could say hi to some of the others.

Sue blew us kisses, Sonnet held up an unidentifiable drawing, Kendra flashed a peace sign, and Lucy pressed her face against the screen so all we saw was pink skin and the corner of one blue eye. I went home that night feeling happy and hopeful.

It was exactly a month after the accident that Biz was moved to a rehab hospital. She was going to be okay, but she had to relearn how to do things like tie her shoes and brush her teeth. Kori stayed with her in Boston, but the rest of the family came home.

The day they arrived, I rode the bus all the way to the store after school and raced inside. Sue was behind the counter helping customers with Deacon. "Hugs later, Maggs," she said. "You're a real champion."

I smiled, then ran to the back and took the stairs two at a

time. Lucy must have heard me because when I reached the top, the door flew open and she jumped into my arms. "We're home!"

Haily pushed past us, her face all bunched up, and stomped all the way down to the store.

"She wants to go see the bf," Lucy whispered. "James said she had to help and then she said she was done helping anyone else forever. It wasn't a very nice thing to say, right, Maggie?"

Inside, Kendra lugged suitcases down the hall and grumbled about James's leg keeping him from doing the grunt work. James was on the phone with Kori, getting a report on Biz's progress since they'd left a few hours before, and Sonnet was at the stove, opening three cans of tomato soup. I set Lucy on the couch and took a suitcase in each hand.

"Where do these go?"

"Green to the moms' room, black to mine."

After my delivery, Sue and Haily were back having a hot discussion in the living room. Haily held her cell phone against her stomach.

"No, you cannot go there. If he wants to help, he can come over here," Sue said. "But we've got a lot of catching up with life to do. No dillydallying."

Lucy climbed onto the arm of the couch so she was taller than the rest of us and jammed her hands onto her hips. "And no smooching!" she said.

The air quit moving. Everyone stopped, everything was

still and quiet. Even the usual rumblings from the store downstairs rested while we held our breaths, waiting for what should have come next. The silence reminded us of what we'd almost lost. Biz wasn't there to repeat Lucy's words. Until she came home, we'd have to get used to it.

Seconds ticked by. Finally, Kendra made mouthing motions with her hand and turned to the stairs.

"Yeah," she said quietly. "No smooching."

TWENTY-EIGHT

My first snowflake fell halfway through November. It was the Sunday before Biz was coming home, and when that first white crystal drifted from the sky, I couldn't help but run outside barefoot to the middle of the field, stretch my arms wide, and lift my face to let a flake land softly on my cheek. It was a sign that things were changing—a beautiful, perfect sign that everything was going to be okay.

Mama threw the kitchen window open and stuck her head out. "Young lady, you get back inside this instant and put your winter clothes on! Haven't you got any sense?" The window slammed shut, but Mama stayed and watched me, all bundled up in the white fox-fur coat Peter had given her for their four-year anniversary. I laughed at her and called out, "We're not in Georgia anymore, Mama, this is what we do in Vermont!" Then I danced around on my tiptoes until they turned red and my ears burned from cold.

The entire Parker family went to Boston on Friday to collect Biz. As soon as school was out, Bob drove me to the store to wait for them. "No sense chugging through town all stop-and-go on the bus," he said. "Besides, we get to talk about cross-country skis!" He shoved his Smart car into gear and we sputtered away.

"I checked in with your mom the other day. She's having fun with the uniform project, eh? Then, get this." He tapped my knee. "She was all ready to go to Boston by herself to get skis as a surprise for you. I had to rein her in and explain you have to be fitted for the right kind of boots, poles, the works. I think I let the air out of her balloon."

"I bet it was more an excuse just to go to Boston. She met some guy online named Jim who lives near there. Are we getting the skis soon?"

"Right after Thanksgiving," he said. "The best place is over near Stowe, and I can't get away until then. Sound good?"

"Sounds good."

It was dark before the family made it home. Deacon did the closing chores in the store, and I went upstairs to heat a casserole that a neighbor had dropped off. I vacuumed the living room and put fresh sheets on the beds in Biz and Lucy's room, then sat on the couch with my hands tucked between my knees, waiting.

After seven weeks in two different hospitals, Biz did not look like Biz when Sue carried her upstairs and set her on the couch next to me. I was totally unprepared. My sweet, chunky Biz wasn't chunky anymore. Her cheeks sank where they used to be plump, and her head had been shaved. Overgrown peach fuzz covered most of it, except where a curved scar on one side looked like a bloodworm crawling across her skin.

She saw my anguish and patted the top of my hand. "I look funny," she said slowly, like a robot. "But I'm okay."

Lucy bounced across the couch, clutching a box of tissues. She stuffed a wad in my hand, and used another to wipe a bit of drool dangling from her sister's lip. "She's gonna be all combobulated again by Christmas," she said cheerfully. "Just you see!"

One side of Biz's mouth curved up and she rolled her eyes. "Not . . . a . . . real word."

Lucy kissed the fuzz on top of her sister's head, jumped from the couch to the coffee table, then to the carpet, and disappeared. Sue put a red walker in the corner and leaned a bright-blue cane against the couch where Biz could reach it. Haily disappeared with her cell phone glued to her ear, and Kendra went straight to the kitchen to complain because the casserole had pork in it.

"Doesn't anyone know how breeding pigs live? They lie

on their sides in metal cages their entire life, being stuffed with food and hormones so they can feed babies who will be slaughtered before they're even a year old. It's gross. And none of you should eat it, either. I'm going to tape a picture of a pig farm on the refrigerator."

Kori tucked a pillow behind Biz's neck, then gave her a lap desk and a tiny blackboard with a brand-new box of colored chalk.

"Occupational therapy," she said. "She's got a ways to go, but we'll get there, right, sweet pea?" She rubbed the back of her hand on Biz's cheek and went off to set the table.

"O-c-c-u-p-p-p-a-a-a . . ." Biz shook her head and pointed to her face. "My mouth doesn't like some words."

Lucy bounced into the room again, lugging an armful of stuffed animals. "Which one do you want?"

Biz pointed to a black and white pony. "Sassy Pants frrrrr." She shook her head violently and scowled.

"Don't try to say it yet," I said.

Sonnet looked up from her sketching by the window. "She's supposed to say everything, otherwise she'll be stagnant in progress." She dipped her head back to her notebook and scratched the pencil across the paper.

Biz leaned her head against my shoulder and looped one arm through mine. Holding out four fingers, she tucked her thumb into her palm.

"My family." She sighed, giving me a squeeze. "Frvrrrr."

I kissed the top of her head. "Forever," I whispered.

I hope.

TWENTY-NINE

On Thanksgiving morning, a new layer of puffy white snow clung to the bare branches of the birch trees. The pony shed in the corner of the field looked like an iced gingerbread house. Mama'd been clattering around in the kitchen since dawn, loud enough to scare off the redbirds gathered at the suet feeder. I went downstairs in search of breakfast, but before I could cross into the kitchen, she handed me the toaster and a package of frozen waffles.

"Out," she said. Her hair flew wild around her face, and flour coated the front of her robe.

"What the heck are you making?"

"It's Thanksgiving, I'm making all kinds of stuff. Go eat in there, I need all the space I can get. Mr. Jim will be here at two."

I stood on the line between the kitchen and family room, toaster and box of frozen waffles in my arms. "Mr. Jim?"

"He's our dinner guest. He's coming up from Boston."

"You're just now telling me this?"

Mama flipped a page in a cookbook and blew a puff of white dust away.

"And here I thought all this was for me."

No answer.

"Am I really supposed to call him Mr. Jim?"

"What else would you call him?"

"I don't know, Mr. Jim is just so, so southern. They don't do that in Vermont. He might not like it."

"Well, he's not from Vermont, he's from Boston and you, Miss Smarty-Pants, don't know a thing about Boston manners, so we're sticking with the Georgia rules. Now scoot. I'm busy."

"Why is he coming?"

"Because it's Thanksgiving and I invited him."

"You told me you weren't looking for another husband."

"I'm not, and don't you sass me. I'm looking for a way to get out of here the very second our obligation is satisfied. Mr. Jim just might be the person to do that."

Tiny hairs on my arms stood on end. "If you're not thinking about marrying him, what do you want him to do?"

"He's interested in buying this place. The entire thing. Cash. On day three hundred and sixty-five. So you be nice. And put on a dress."

I stood frozen in that spot, something horrible filling my body. I was too late. I'd waited too long to speak up. Mama didn't know I wanted to stay in Vermont. I should have shouted, not hinted. Lights danced in front of my eyes. The room filled with a purple glow and I was back in the woods again. The smell of earth rose in the air as I ran past maples and caught the sunlight glinting off rusted buckets hanging from the trees. His voice surrounded me.

"Someday, Magnolia Grace, these woods will belong to you."

I blinked hard. Mama's head was bent over the cookbook, her index finger running left to right as she read something out loud to herself.

"No," I said firmly.

She looked up, her eyes wide. "Excuse me? No what?"

I squeezed the toaster and waffle box tighter. "I don't want to sell the farm, Mama. I want to stay here."

"Pffff. What kind of nonsense are you thinking of?" she said, turning back to her cookbook. "Why on earth would we stay here when we'll be able to live anywhere we want? Now go on. I'm busy."

"No!" I said, louder. Her head jerked up. "It's my farm and we're not selling it."

"What has gotten into you?"

The toaster and box of waffles clattered to the floor. Leftover crumbs spilled across polished wood. Mama's face exploded into more shades of red than I knew existed. I left her standing there with her mouth half open, ran up the stairs, and slammed my bedroom door so hard the lamp rattled. She didn't follow. Ten minutes later, I was making tracks through the iced woods, running all the way to the sugar shack. Inside, I planted my face and arms on the table and let loose a thousand tears. The day had come when I had to fight for my daddy's farm, and I'd already lost round one. I felt hopelessly unprepared.

At exactly two o'clock a shiny black car pulled into the driveway. Mama hadn't said one word about the morning's incident, which made me feel as important as the discarded plastic wrapper she'd peeled off a grocery store pie.

"He's here," I said. "Oh, yippee . . ."

She pushed past me and thrust an apron in my hands, then fluffed her hair in front of the hall mirror. "Hide that, sugar, and be polite."

I went to wait on the window seat in the living room. There was some kind of fuss in the hallway when the famous Mr. Jim came inside. Mama oohed and aahed, they both laughed, the coat closet opened and closed, and then there they were, standing side by side, staring at me. Mama held a massive bouquet of orange and yellow lilies in her arms.

"Jim, this is my daughter," she said. She leaned close to

him and whispered, "The one I told you about."

I stood up. "Hello," I said. It was all I could manage.

Mr. Jim crossed the room and took my hand. "Hello, ah, I'm sorry, I didn't get your name."

"It's Magnolia Grace, sir, but you can call me Maggie," I said.

"Lovely," he said. "And please, call me Jim. Up here in the North, it makes us feel old to be called sir."

As much as I wanted to hate him, I couldn't help noticing his eyes crinkled at the corners like Kori's, and they were every bit as blue as Lucy's.

"Thank you."

The three of us stood silently in this awkward circle, Jim watching my face, Mama watching him watch me, and me feeling like I was on display in a freak museum.

Jim held out a white gift bag. "A token of appreciation for having me spend this special day with you and your mother."

Mama pushed the bag into my hands. "Go ahead, sweetheart, open it."

Inside were two books. The first one was full of glossy, color photos of the flora and fauna of New England. The second was a tiny green volume of poems with ivory pages edged in gold.

"It's Robert Frost," Jim said, his face all shiny and bright. "He lived here, you know, in Vermont. There's a farm in Shaftesbury, and he spent a lot of time in Ripton, near Middlebury. Have you been there yet?"

"No, sir. Sorry, I mean Jim."

Mama fluttered her hands around her face. "I told him how much you like to read, sugar, and how you were always wanting to go to the library to look up things about Vermont trees and such. He said he knew just what to bring you, isn't that right, Jim?"

A) I'd only asked her to take me to the library once, and B) I didn't want Jim to give me a thoughtful gift. He was only trying to butter me up. That nixed anything nice about him, crinkly blue eyes, or books of birds and poetry.

I tilted my chin up. "Thank you so much."

Another uncomfortable pause. Mama got nervous and started talking too fast.

"Jim, could you build us a nice fire while I get the hors d'oeuvres ready? I think I got all the necessary ingredients. For the fire I mean. The hors d'oeuvres are done. We didn't have any need for a fireplace in the South, as you might imagine. Precious, you stay back now while Mr. Jim does that. Oh, look, the redbirds are back—they flew away this morning. We love the redbirds, don't we, sugar? I'm sure there'll be all sorts of information about them in that pretty new book of yours."

She flitted away to get the hors d'oeuvres. I settled in to watch Jim build a fire like it was the most interesting thing I'd ever seen, but really, I was silently plotting my next move.

THIRTY

J im sliced a shiny knife into the breast of the bird.

"This turkey is magnificent!"

"It's fresh killed, from a real turkey farm on the way to Burlington. I drove all the way there on Monday to get it. Sugar, pass me the dressing, please."

Jim had never had sweet potato casserole or green bean casserole, and he called dressing "stuffing" because, he said, before people knew about turkey and salmonella it used to be cooked inside the bird. Like stuffed into that big hole when the bird was still raw. They talked about polite things while we ate, and after we finished with the turkey and dressing and potatoes and casseroles and cranberries and all the rest, Mama brought in a pecan pie and held it out like a prize.

"I had the pecans shipped special from Georgia."

It wasn't one hundred percent a lie. She'd taken the grocery store pie and topped it with pecans that came in a package with *Georgia* written across the front, then added butter and brown sugar and baked it long enough for everything to glaze together. She went off to get coffee, but I kept my mouth shut, waiting, like a tiger, to be poked. For the plan I'd come up with to work, it had to be Mr. Jim who did the poking.

He didn't make the tiger wait very long.

"So, Maggie, do you think you'll move back to Georgia right away? Or perhaps take some time to travel a bit first?"

I slipped the triangular pie server underneath the crust and lifted a piece heavy with pecans onto a dessert plate. "Excuse me?"

Mama hustled back to the table with a tray of china cups and saucers. "We haven't decided exactly where we'll go yet, but I think we've definitely ruled out Kentucky."

"Kentucky would be good if you were a horse person, I suppose. Do you like horses?"

I laid my fork down and made sure my eyes grew big and wide. "I don't know what you're talking about."

Jim chuckled and took a cup of coffee from Mama. "You don't know what I mean about the horses?"

"No, I mean about Georgia. We're not moving back to Georgia, we're staying here."

Jim held his cup halfway to his mouth. Mama spilled coffee on the white tablecloth.

"My daddy left me this farm—didn't Mama tell you? I didn't get to know him growing up, and now he's dead, so it's really good we get to live here because I can learn things about him, and since my stepfather turned out to be gay and all, Mama doesn't want to go back to Atlanta anyway. So we're staying put right here."

I dug my fork into the pecan pie. Mama's face was frozen.

"Sweetheart, if I didn't know you better, I'd think you were being impertinent."

"Did I say something wrong? I'm sorry, I didn't mean to. He just thought we were moving back to Georgia next year and I was explaining to him why we're staying here on the farm."

Her head swayed the tiniest bit, like she was balancing to keep it from exploding off her shoulders. First her eyes bulged, then they narrowed into tiny slits, and her fingers curled tight around her fork.

"I am sure you know perfectly well we are not staying here," she said. She glanced quickly at Mr. Jim. He looked like he wanted to be anyplace but at our dinner table. "We will continue this discussion after our guest has left. Jim, would you like cream for your coffee?"

"No, thank you, Dee, I'm a black coffee guy."

"Yes, of course you are."

"You told me specifically that we were not moving back to

Georgia, that there wasn't anything there for us anymore, remember?"

"Of course I remember, but there was no discussion about staying here on this farm. Ever." She turned to Mr. Jim. "I'm so sorry, Jim, she doesn't know what she's saying."

"I *do* know what I'm saying," I said firmly. "And I want to stay here."

"We are not going to discuss this silly notion in front of company. Now eat your dessert. I always did like that rule about how children should be seen and not heard."

"We should discuss it in front of Jim, because that's why he's here, right? So you can make me like him, so I won't care when he comes with cash on day three hundred and sixty-five. Isn't that what you told me?"

Mama's face tightened so much I thought her skin might pop.

"Whoa, whoa, whoa, ladies, let's not get into a fight," Jim said. "I am interested in this farm, Maggie—who wouldn't be, it's magnificent. But we don't have to talk about this here and now. We have seven months to make a decision."

He reached out to pat my hand like I was a puppy. I jerked away.

"It won't be for sale in seven months, either."

Mama shot up from her chair, gripping the side of the table so hard her knuckles turned white. "You. Are. Excused!" She flung her arm in the direction of the stairs.

"Fine!" I yelled. "But this farm was my daddy's and it's

the only thing I have of him, so don't even think for one second that I'm changing my mind!"

I fled the room and pounded up the stairs, making sure every footstep was heard all over the entire state. Tossing my denim skirt on the floor, I yanked on a pair of jeans and fumbled through tears and shaking hands to zip them up. My stomach felt like a piece of wire was twisted around it. I grabbed two sweatshirts, layered one on top of the other, and tiptoed down the back stairs and out into the cold.

The sun sank quickly. The temperature dropped so fast I could see my own breath by the time I got to the Parkers'. I leaned against Deacon's truck in the driveway and shivered in the dark. A single candle flickered from each of the second-floor windows, one in the kitchen, two in the living room, and one in Sue and Kori's bedroom. Laughter and voices drifted down, mingling with the smell of pumpkin pie and fresh snow. The middle of my chest squeezed so tight it was hard to breathe. Kendra was right; I was an outsider. I didn't belong to this family, and I'd never felt it as much as I did right then.

A face appeared in one of the windows. Sonnet pulled a sheer curtain aside and watched me watching her, then let the curtain fall again and moved away. I wiped my eyes with the sleeve of my sweatshirt. As much as I couldn't stand the thought of going home, if I stood out in the cold much longer, my tears would freeze as soon as they hit my cheeks.

I'd just turned toward the road when Sue came around

from the side of the house. I heard her feet crunch on the driveway, and saw her walking toward me with her arms spread wide. Uncontrollable sobs exploded from my chest.

"Hey, Maggie, you all right, hon?"

She pulled me into a hug and planted my face on her shoulder.

"Oh, boy, oh boy. Good old holidays. Always inspiration for drama."

Hiccup. Hiccup.

I looked up. "Mama and I had such a big fight at dinner."

"Of course you did." She brushed wet hair out of my face and smiled. "We've already had two fights with Haily, and Kendra and Lucy got into it in a big way. You'll be able to tell by the gravy splattered on the ceiling. Holidays are tough, hon."

I nodded and sniffled, but I didn't want to let go of her. She jiggled my shoulder.

"Hey, what kind of pie do you like? We spent most of yesterday and this morning baking. Pumpkin, cherry, pecan, mincemeat, blueberry—I think that's it. Nope, we have buttermilk pie, too. We love pie. Let's go get some, okay?"

Minutes later I was warm and toasty in the living room above the country store, eating pie smothered in whipped cream with Biz snuggled up to my side, watching Deacon and the others play charades. At the end of one game, James leaned over and inspected the top of Biz's head.

"Hey, look at that! Your hair's coming in bright red, just like mine!"

Biz stiffened and there was a beat of silence before she reached up and touched the new threads sticking straight toward the ceiling.

"No, it's not!"

Everyone laughed together, and my whole world tilted. I wanted to reach out and touch all the smiling faces around me. I wanted to say that I loved them, every one of them, and I wished I could make that moment last forever. But, of course, I didn't say anything. I pulled Biz closer and leaned my cheek against the yellow fuzz that announced she was getting better. Someone handed me another piece of pie, and a new game started up.

THIRTY-ONE

Jim's car turned out of the driveway just as Deacon and I rounded the bend a little after eight. Deacon cut the truck lights and pulled slowly up to the house.

"You want me to come in with you?"

I could see Mama through the windows, moving between the counter and the sink in the kitchen. She might not even know I'd left. So different from the Parkers. I touched my cheek, remembering the way Kori had cupped her hand under my chin before I'd left and said, "I'm glad you came to us, Maggs. It was a good Thanksgiving."

"I'm okay. But thanks."

Deacon patted my shoulder. "You know where to find me and Quince."

I got out and fumbled my way around to the back of the house in the dark.

For Mama and me, the way we'd always acted when there had been an "unpleasantness"—which was the way she referred to out-and-out fights—was to pretend nothing had happened. This might not have changed for her, but I couldn't let it go. My heartache was real. I'd stuffed too much down inside my whole life; there was no room for more.

The morning after Thanksgiving, I wrapped up in the new red parka she'd bought me and snuck out to the barn before she was awake. I hadn't been back to see the magnolias for a while, but on this day, with a showdown between the two of us in clear view, I needed more than courage. I needed a reminder of what I'd missed out on, and why I wanted so badly to stay.

I folded the big tarp into a square on the floor and lined the paintings up against the wall, smallest to biggest, left to right, and sat cross-legged to study them. What did he feel when he stroked his brush across the canvas? Did he paint each one on my actual birthday? Or did he work on them over the winter, before sugaring season took all his time? I dabbed my fingertip on the unfinished painting, right where my eyes would have been, and pretended to color them sky blue. It was nice being up here by myself, almost like he was sitting beside me, so close I could smell the Listerine on his breath. I remembered that now—that he always smelled like Listerine when he hugged me.

The barn door rolled open downstairs.

"Sugar?"

I crawled out to the landing and peered over the edge. Mama stood in the middle of the big empty first floor in her fur coat and pink snow boots, looking like she was lost on a trek to Antarctica.

"I'm up here."

She startled. "Oh! I saw you come out. What are you doing?"

"I like it in here."

"Your daddy used to come here to paint."

"I know. Some of them are in this room."

"Still? I figured he'd sold them all. People loved those landscapes." She lifted the collar up around her ears and shivered. "It's so cold in this barn. It's a wonder Jesus survived his birth."

"These aren't just landscapes," I said. "Some are different."

"Different?"

I'd spoken too soon. I wasn't ready to share the magnolias with her, and now she'd want to see them. Thoughts flew through my mind so fast I couldn't catch them. What should I say? How could I use this in the Stay-in-Vermont Action Plan?

"He painted magnolias," I said bluntly.

"Magnolias?" She climbed the steps. Her pink boots left wet marks on the wood. "I didn't know that."

When she got to the top I moved between her and the room where the magnolias were still lined up against the walls. "I didn't know he painted anything. I had to find out from two girls at school," I said.

She heard the accusation in my tone and stopped, guarded. "May I see them?" she asked quietly.

Reluctant but hopeful at the same time, I led her to the room. Maybe seeing them would make her understand why it was so important to me to stay. Her eyes moved slowly from one painting to the next, her mouth dropping open slightly. When she got to the last one, she raised a hand toward the faceless image, then jerked it away.

"Do you know who that is?" I asked.

"Of course I do," she said gently. "They're beautiful. He even remembered the way your eyelashes had that little bit of gold on the end. I never knew he painted these."

"Neither did I." My voice wobbled. I was trying so hard to sound certain, and grown-up, but everything inside trembled. "Why didn't I get to know him when he was alive?"

Her eyes softened again, the way they'd been that night I asked about the divorce. "It was complicated, sugar. He came to Georgia once, don't you remember?"

I nodded. "But why only once? Every time I asked about him, you made me feel like I didn't appreciate Peter and should stop asking."

"Peter took good care of you. He gave you everything you needed."

I shook my head. "No, he didn't. He gave me *things*. You gave me *things*. We never talked about stuff that mattered. You made me feel ashamed whenever I asked questions about my own daddy."

"How do you think Peter would have felt if he knew you were asking all those questions when he did everything for you? He took you in as his own when we married, without question. Have you ever considered his feelings?"

That tipped me over the edge. "I don't really care how he felt," I yelled. "The man who painted these pictures was my father!"

Mama's eyes got big and her nostrils flared, the same way Sassy Pants's did when she got spooked. "This, young lady, is exactly why we never discuss this sort of thing. Get your hysteria under control. This is not how we behave."

She turned and stalked toward the door, but I couldn't let it go. "Maybe that's the way we did it before, but we aren't in Georgia anymore!"

She wheeled around, her face frozen in a scary, fake-smile, wild-eyed expression. "Oh. I. Am. Aware," she snapped. "Now come down out of this place. Your real *mother* is taking you shopping at the Black Friday sales."

THIRTY-TWO

The night before school started again, Mama did the unthinkable. She broke her own golden rule, right in the middle of dinner.

"Sugar," she said, her eyes trained on a mound of mashed potatoes, "I want to talk to you about Mr. Jim and what happened on Thanksgiving."

I nearly choked on my milk.

"I think it's important you understand something," she said.

"There isn't anything to understand."

"Yes, there is, and I need you to hear me out. I know you think you want to stay here, but it isn't something I ever considered. We're only required to be here—"

I interrupted her. "I want to know about my daddy."

She sat back in her chair. "Right now?"

I nodded.

"Do you think that will help you get over this obsession about staying here?"

"It's not an obsession. And it's two separate things, anyway."

"Not really. If this wasn't your daddy's farm, you'd have no interest in staying. I understand that, but it doesn't mean it's the right choice for us."

"I didn't even know him. The kids at school know more about him than I do. It's embarrassing."

"Okay, I can tell you some things. He was creative. He was estranged from his family. When we found out you were coming, he joined the military without even discussing it with me. He thought it was the best way to support us."

She got up and pretended to look for something in the cabinets, slapping the doors shut after inspecting each one.

"Tell me something real."

She twirled around. "Real? What's not real about those things?"

"What was he like? What made him happy?"

"Do we really have to do this?"

Something told me not to say a word, that if I forced her to talk first, she'd tell me. I chewed the inside of my lip and waited until she sat down.

"Okay, if you must know, there was the before person, and

the after. Before he went to Afghanistan he loved to paint. He loved being outside, he loved trees. He picked wildflowers and kept them in a jar. He was the only man I ever knew who read poetry books in public, and sometimes he read out loud to me. Is this the kind of stuff you mean?"

The image of my daddy reading a poem to a younger version of Mama spread warmth throughout my body. She was telling me stuff I'd waited a lifetime to hear.

"Please keep going."

"He wouldn't talk much about his family. I'm not sure what happened, but he didn't like them. He said they were judgmental. He only wore Levi's jeans because his legs were so long and they fit him the best. He could build anything with wood. He had those kind of eyes people say are soulful. Never raised his voice. He had huge hands that were gentle and soft. And he smiled all the time."

"What about after?"

Her voice got quiet. "There was barely any shadow of him left. I knew it as soon as we met him up here. He needed to be alone most of the time. You made him happy, but he reminded me of a turtle. He'd poke his head out for a few hours and do things with you, then he'd disappear for days. And I don't mean literally disappear—he was here, but his head was somewhere else. He couldn't stand noise. Sometimes he thought he was back in the war. And sometimes he could get violent. It was frightening."

"Did he have PTSD?"

"How do you know about PTSD?"

"Because I went to school and they taught us stuff."

"Okay, yes, he had PTSD."

"And that's why we left?"

"That's why we left."

"But he only came to see me one time."

"I'm sure he wanted to come more, sugar, but he was crippled by this problem. It was almost impossible for him to travel."

"Why didn't you bring me up here?"

Little creases bunched on her forehead. Her mouth moved like Biz's when she tried to make uncooperative words come out. Finally, her eyes got really big and she said, "Don't you see? He had a mental illness. Mental!"

"Why does that mean you couldn't bring me?"

"PTSD is an adult problem. Children shouldn't be exposed to those kinds of things."

"It's not like he had chicken pox, or a cold I could catch."

"You were safe in Atlanta, sugar. Peter may not have been your biological father, but he was stable. Your daddy's illness was unpredictable. He was damaged. Who knows what kind of lasting effect being around him could have had on you!"

"But you never gave me a choice. You should have done something to make it happen and now it's too late."

"You were too young to know how to make that kind of decision."

My voice had risen to a semihysterical level, but I wasn't

finished. I had so much more to say. "I belong here. I was always supposed to be here. You should have brought me. It's your fault! He wanted me here. He missed me so much he had to paint me! Is that the lasting effect you were worried about? He would never have let anything bad happen. He told me."

Mama's eyes got really big. "When could he have possibly said that to you?"

"I—I'm not sure, I don't know, I just know he did. He promised. I remember."

She put her hands against the edge of the table and stood up, her voice cold and shaky.

"We're not discussing this anymore. It never ends well."

On Monday I stayed on the bus past our house after school and rode to the store with Lucy, Kendra, and Sonnet. My heart still hurt from the fight the night before, and I didn't have the energy to face Mama. Sue was waiting in the driveway with the car engine running.

"You three have dentist appointments," she said to the girls. "Come with me."

"Dentist?"

"I don't want to go to the dentist!"

"You're going, so get in the car," she said. "Maggie, maybe you could help Kori. Biz has the physical therapist with her. She's a little self-conscious. Givin' her some space."

Sonnet was the only one who didn't argue about the

dentist. She slipped into the front seat while Sue practically had to push the other two in the back. By the time they drove off, poor little Lucy was crying, her red face pressed against the back window.

When the bell over the door binged, Kori looked up from where she was kneeling on the floor and smiled. "Hey, Maggs, how are things?"

"Okay, sort of," I said. "Sue said you might need help."

"Sure, I can always use an extra hand. We're still playing catch-up. Christmas stuff needs to get out."

I tossed my backpack behind the counter and knelt beside her, packing dozens of tins of maple syrup with plain labels into boxes. The new cans we were putting on the shelves had a sprig of holly painted above a picture of a sleigh and two big horses standing by a sugar shack. My sugar shack.

"Didn't my daddy paint stuff like this?"

She smiled and nodded. "Except for the holly, that's his painting."

"Is this my sugar shack?"

"Might be, they all kind of look alike to me, except the great big ones. His original painting is hanging in the bank in town."

I'd never thought about his artwork being in places where I could go see it, I only knew about the boxes upstairs in the barn.

"I found a painting he did called *The Georgia View*."

"I know that one. When the weather was good, that was

189

your dad's favorite place to paint. He said on a clear day he could see all the way to Georgia. Hence, the name."

"Do you know about the magnolias?"

"I do. They're lovely."

"Mama says he was damaged and unpredictable."

Kori knelt in front of me and lifted my chin. "He was a good man, Maggs. He had some challenges, but he was a truly good man."

"Did he try to get better? From the PTSD, I mean."

Kori paused just long enough for me to know the answer before she said anything. "He worked really hard, but I'd be lying if I said he was completely over it. It's a process. He used art therapy to control his anxiety, and that was huge. He was definitely better, but not fixed."

"She didn't bring me to see him because she didn't think I should be exposed to him, but I wish I'd known him more."

"I know for a fact that he wished the same thing."

The softness in her face made me feel safe. And she'd said he was a good man. That made my whole body fill up with happy.

"Thank you," I said. "I'm glad I came here today."

"Me, too."

THIRTY-THREE

The next Friday, Bob and Angela took me to Stowe to buy cross-country skis. Mama gave me the credit card and told them she wasn't feeling well, but she was faking it. The real truth was she didn't want them to see the Grand Canyon of distance between the two of us. It was bad enough that it could require explaining.

On Saturday I had my first ski lesson, which was perfect timing because I desperately needed to laugh. Those ten-mile-long sticks attached to my feet gave us plenty of opportunity. At least a handful of times one of them crossed over the other and I tumbled sideways into the snow. Bob showed me once how to get up on my own, then refused to help again.

"You've got to learn now, or you'll never able to go out alone," he said.

By Sunday afternoon I was able to successfully glide across the field without falling. I took my very first selfie and emailed it to Angela with a note that said, *Done!*

The minute I got off the bus every day, I strapped on those skis and headed out. The first time I went to the sugar shack, I came home with a bruised body and a sore ego after crashing into multiple rocks and tree stumps hidden under the snow. But it was worth every aching muscle; every bit of near-frost-bitten skin; and every damp, stinky sock I stripped off at night.

Mama and I came to a temporary truce. We ate dinner with the TV on so we didn't have to talk. We steered clear of conversations that might include the word *daddy* or *Vermont*. She left the catalog of school uniforms out on the kitchen table, with colored sticky notes marking specific pages, and went to Burlington once to get samples, but I only knew that because Bob told me.

The day the first load of Christmas trees was delivered to the country store, James gave me a pair of thick deerskin gloves.

"Mark your initials inside," he said. "We each have a pair, but you don't want Haily nabbing them. She loses hers all the time."

I smiled the rest of that day.

We organized the trees by type and size, and spread open the limbs of the best ones to stand upright in the middle of the temporary lot between the store and the road. Haily and Ethan Edward strung hundreds of white lights so everyone driving by knew the trees had arrived. Deacon put up a tent with a table, chairs, and a giant heater that blew hot air where customers could come in out of the cold and drink spiced cider. White lattice panels displayed evergreen wreaths with red holly berries, and bundles of mistletoe hung overhead from strings. Biz and Lucy giggled every time someone walked under them.

"Don't let Haily and Ethan Edward stand there," Lucy said. "They'll kiss!"

"Yeah," said Biz. "They'll kiss." She puckered her lips and made a loud sucking noise.

Lucy bit into a cookie and giggled so hard she spewed crumbs everywhere.

Kendra walked past with an urn of hot cider. "Do you really think they need mistletoe?"

I loved being at the tree lot. It vibrated with energy and happiness. I loved the smells of the evergreens and the cars full of people who came to pick out their trees. I loved that I was important to the Parker family, and every time a customer recognized me as "one of them," my heart grew a little bigger.

* * *

After ten days, Mama'd had enough of the truce. She showed up at the store all smiles, carting along a gold bag full of tiny wrapped gifts for Sue and Kori. Sonnet came to the tent where I was helping Biz catch up on missed schoolwork. We were learning the state names.

"Your mother's in the store," Sonnet said. "She wants you to pick out a tree with her."

Biz pushed herself up from her chair. The map and colored pencils scattered across the table. "I wanna see her! I bet she's all dressed up!"

Lucy raced past her. "I'm coming, too!"

By the time I got inside, Lucy's arms circled Mama's hips, and Biz was letting her touch her hair, which still stuck out like the fuzzy glow from an old lightbulb.

"She's getting a tree! Can we help her pick?" Lucy begged Kori.

"Of course you can, Lu, the trees are right outside. It's not like you're taking a trip to Canada."

"You do want me to help you, right?"

Mama bent down and touched the end of Lucy's nose with her fingertip. Her nails were painted Christmas red.

"Why do you think I came here?"

"They're outside, come on," Lucy said, slipping her blue-mittened hand into Mama's.

Biz went to the other hand. "I'm helping, too."

"Well, now that I have two beautiful escorts," Mama said, "let's go buy us a tree!"

They stopped at the blue spruce first, then the white pine, and finally the Fraser firs.

"Blue spruce grow in Canada—that's why they cost more," Lucy said, imitating the words I'd heard a dozen times. "Pines grow here, but they aren't as strong for holding up heavy ornaments."

Biz wagged a finger. "I bet you don't like a mess, so maybe you should pick a Fraser fir. They don't shed."

Kori handed Mama a cup of hot cider. "They've got quite the sales pitch going."

"It's the truth," Lucy insisted.

"It isn't a pitch if it's one hundred percent truth!" Biz said.

Mama tilted her face to the sky and laughed. Her perfect white teeth sparkled under the twinkling lights. "Well now, my sweet girls, aren't you just the smartest things ever," she said, pouring on her thickest southern accent.

Biz tilted her head back like Mama had and laughed. "Ever," she said with a bunch of *y*'s strung through the middle.

Lucy watched her sister and imitated her. "Ever."

I wished I felt the same fascination for Mama as the girls, but everything she did annoyed me. And that prickly little thought made me wonder why I'd never gotten this mama before, why she'd saved all this motherly charm for Biz and Lucy. Wasn't I good enough? Or did she think maybe I, too, was damaged?

She ended up picking the fattest blue spruce on the lot.

"We never had one like this in Georgia, isn't that right, sugar?"

We had a fake tree in Georgia. Clarissa put it up *and* decorated it for us. I kept my mouth shut.

"It's so exciting to have something new!"

"Blue spruce are my favorite," Lucy said.

"No, they're not," claimed Biz. "You don't even like the way they smell."

Lucy's face bunched up. "You're lying!"

"Am not," Biz snarled.

Lucy lunged forward, both arms outstretched, ready to push her sister to the ground. I dived in between and blocked what could have set Biz's physical therapy back by months. Kori grabbed Lucy's arms from behind.

"You girls behave or Maggie's mom won't come visit anymore."

"Well, I don't condone a tussle between sisters, but it's not every day a gal has two beautiful girls fighting over her. I can see why my own daughter prefers being here than at home."

Her words sliced through the air like a steel blade. Kori looked at me quickly. Her expression said *Let it go.*

James promised to deliver the tree the next evening and set it up with Deacon. Then Mama dropped a bomb.

"I've never had a tree-decorating party," she said. Biz and Lucy stared up at her, their eyes wide, their hands practically quivering. "Would y'all come over Friday night? Seven o'clock? Deacon, too. And Quince. I'll make cookies and we'll have music and by the end of the night, we'll have the prettiest tree in all of Vermont!"

"We'd love to come," Kori said. "I'm sure Haily and Ethan Edward won't mind staying behind for an hour. They can join us after closing. If that's okay for Ethan Edward to come."

Mama clapped her hands together. "Of course! Ethan Edward is welcome, too!"

"He's Haily's bf," Lucy said.

"That means boyfriend," Biz said. "He gave her a—"

"Okay!" I said, clapping my hands loudly. "Let's go! Come on, Mama, time to go home."

I pulled her by the sleeve across the lot to the driveway before Biz could say any more about the still-famous hickey. When I looked back, James was holding his hand over her mouth, and the whole family was laughing.

On the way home I initiated the first conversation Mama and I'd had in over a week.

"Are you insane? You realize there are six kids, right? So that's eight people you've just invited, plus Deacon and Quince and Ethan Edward. We don't own a cookie cutter, and you left all the ornaments in Georgia, remember? How are we going to eat Christmas cookies and decorate a tree without those things?"

Her forehead stitched together in the center. "I don't know just yet, but I'll figure it out."

I sank down in my seat and prayed for a massive, road-closing snowstorm to hit Vermont within the next seventy-two hours.

THIRTY-FOUR

No great snowstorm swooped through to save me, but by Friday night I was sure Mama'd sworn off doing anything so impulsive again. She spent two days driving all over the state in search of unique Christmas ornaments so it looked like they'd been collected over many years. Somehow she'd even scrounged up a glazed ceramic peach with *CHRISTMAS IN GEORGIA* written across the front from a thrift store. She held it up proudly.

"No one will ever suspect we didn't have ornaments until today!"

"Except most of these are in brand-new boxes. That might be a clue."

She glanced around the kitchen, then scurried off. By dinnertime, all evidence of her shopping spree had disappeared, and each ornament was wrapped in a piece of tissue, hand-crinkled by Mama.

Friday afternoon the kitchen smelled of smoke, and not the kind that came from a fireplace. This was definitely a burned-food odor. Platters of near-perfect gingerbread men and sugar cookies lined the counter. I scouted around, looking for the source. Nothing obvious until I opened the trash can lid. The entire thing was full of scorched-black stars, trees, and gingerbread men.

"Wow," I said. "Just wow."

I hauled the bag outside and hid it, then lit some scented candles in the kitchen. Hopefully the squirrels would eat cookies that were only ashes held together by charred sugar.

At ten till seven, Mama cornered me. "Now, is there anything I should do differently or say differently tonight?"

"What do you mean?"

"These people are your friends, sweetheart. I've never entertained a gay couple before. I mean, other than Peter. Help me, I don't want to say something stupid and embarrass you."

"Same-sex marriage became legal in Vermont in 2009, Mama, and it was the first state to allow civil unions between same-sex couples long before that. People here don't care, and neither should you."

"I *don't* care, not the way you're suggesting. I'm doing this for you. And where did you learn all that stuff, anyway?"

"At my cushy, conservative private school in Atlanta, all the way back in fourth grade. Seriously, sometimes you act like you've been living under a rock."

Her mouth dropped open and her eyes welled up.

"Okay, okay, I'm sorry," I said quickly. "I didn't mean to sound like that, but they're just people. Treat them like you want to be treated, like you always tell me to do."

She started bawling, right there in the kitchen. "Now look, my face is going to be red and splotchy when they get here!"

I grabbed a tissue box and gave it to her. "It's nothing to cry about."

"Maybe for you, but sometimes you make me feel so inadequate, even when I'm trying so hard—"

The doorbell rang three times in a row. I'd been antsy for them to get here so Mama and I didn't have to be alone, but she'd actually just said something real, something from her heart, about feelings. Something I could build on.

"Oh no, they're here." She smoothed her dress and threw the tissue away. "Do I look okay?"

She looked pathetic. "I think Biz and Lucy are hoping for the movie star Mama, so maybe you want to go clean the mascara off your face. Other than that, you look great."

The doorbell rang again. A tiny hand knocked on the window. Mama ran up the stairs and I went to greet our guests.

She came down a few minutes later, all charm and ho-ho-ho. Lucy's and Biz's eyes got really big when they saw her decked out in her fancy red Christmas outfit, complete with glittery earrings and a green and gold scarf. They ran to her for hugs, and she burst into tears again and fled. The rest of us stood in that tiny front room, which now had the giant blue spruce taking up a quarter of the space, and watched her run off.

"What did we do?" Biz asked.

"Nothing," I said.

Kori touched my shoulder. "Do you need to go help her?"

"No, she'll be fine."

Silently, we sorted through the ornaments, pulling them out of the fake-used boxes, while James and Sue circled the tree with lights.

"Where are the cookies?" Lucy asked.

"Shhhhh," Kendra said. "Don't be rude."

"It's not rude—she said we'd have cookies."

"I'll get them," I said.

"Let's wait for your mom," Kori said. "She went to a lot of trouble for us."

Ten minutes later Mama swept back in smelling of hairspray and potpourri perfume. She gathered Biz and Lucy into her arms. "I'm so sorry, my sweet precious girls. I had an emotional moment of gratitude. I'm so happy y'all are here."

"Is gratitude an emotion?" Lucy asked.

Mama kissed her cheek. "Well, it sure as heck made me emotional. Now, let's get this party started. How about you girls help me bring in some cookies?"

"Yeah!"

"I can carry a tray by myself," Biz said. "Watch." She stood tall, held her arms out to the side, and walked a straight line without any hint of a limp or bobble.

The three of them went off to the kitchen, and the rest of us all sighed at the same time. Sonnet sat at the piano and let her fingers graze the tops of the ivory keys, her back straight, her shiny black hair lying flat past her waist.

"He used to let me play," she said. "I came here for lessons because we only have a keyboard."

Mama came around the corner with a pitcher of eggnog, trailed by Lucy and Biz, who each carried a platter piled high with cookies. My heart tweaked again. They'd had more fun with her in those few minutes than I remembered having in my whole life. Mama poured eggnog and the little girls went around the room offering cookies to everyone.

"She taught us how to do it," Biz whispered.

Mama set a cup on the piano for Sonnet. "Would you play for us?" she asked.

Sonnet's fingers flowed across the piano keys like they belonged there. The music settled everything down as we ate cookies and dug through boxes. Mama was right smack in the middle of it, telling stories about each ornament. She was so theatrical, if I hadn't seen them arrive just the other day, I would have loved the history behind each and every one. Except that she was lying to my friends. I did not love that part.

Haily and Ethan Edward arrived with Deacon. Somehow

we scrunched all those people into that little front room and for a while, the evening was jolly. Then Haily pulled out the Georgia peach and held it up.

"Ooooo, I like this. Do you have one of the magnolias?"

The music stopped. Mama froze, her hand in the air holding up a glittery snowflake.

"A magnolia?" I asked.

"The ones Johnny Austin made. We each have one. Didn't he send one to you?"

Magnolias symbolize strength, perseverance, dignity, a love of nature," he'd said. Then he cupped his hands. Cradled inside was a beautiful wood ornament. "There won't be any magnolias in Vermont until you come back."

He'd given it to me in Georgia, but I had no memory of seeing it after that day. "He gave me one. But I don't know where it is."

"It's in your box," Mama said quickly.

"My box? What box?"

A piece of silver tinsel drifted from Mama's hair. Her eyes pleaded with me. *Not now.*

"Where we keep his letters, remember?"

"What letters?"

"Did I say something wrong?" Haily asked.

Mama startled, like she'd forgotten anyone else was there except the two of us. "No, no, it's not you. Christmas is such a . . . it's our first here all alone, and our first party. I feel a little clumsy, I'm sorry."

She was lying again. There was no box and we both knew it. What had she done with the ornament? Had she hidden it away because it wasn't all glittery and shiny like her others? Is that the real reason we'd left, because she wanted a husband who was polished and all in one piece?

"Mama's not used to serving guests by herself," I said bitterly. "She only knows how to be a rich man's wife."

When I saw the look on Kori's face, I wished I could take the words back and swallow them. She was shocked and sad and disappointed in me. She was the last person on earth I ever wanted to disappoint.

"I'm sorry—"

Mama interrupted. "That's the truth, though—she's right."

Even after what I'd said, she was sticking up for me.

"But here I am, giving it a go. You should have seen all the cookies I burned this afternoon. What a mess! I'm just lucky we have such patient guests for my trial run."

"What's a trial run?"

"You're not running."

I ducked my head and pushed past them to escape before tears exploded from my eyes, but I didn't get out before I heard Mama say, "It means we did things differently in Georgia. I'm trying to learn new rules. The Vermont rules."

I didn't go to the tree lot the next day, even though it was Saturday. I was too ashamed to face anyone, and too angry with Mama to even go downstairs when she was around. I was mad at her for so many things, including the way she stuck up for me after I'd been so mean.

It was dark when the doorbell rang that evening. I looked out the upstairs window and saw James's truck idling in the driveway, then ran back to my room and shut the door. Five minutes later my phone beeped. It was a text with a picture of Lucy standing in our front hallway, holding a whole pie in her hands.

Do you think we don't have fights at our house? Leaving the pie for tonight. See you at the lot tomorrow.

I put the phone down and laid my head on the pillow. A minute later the phone beeped again.

Lu says to tell you it's blueberry, as blue as her eyes.

THIRTY-FIVE

The Tuesday before Christmas break, Mama said she had to go to Boston for a couple of days and I would be staying with Kori and Sue. The word *Boston* made me think instantly of Mr. Jim. My stomach soured. I didn't even lift my head from my homework.

"Fine with me."

I hadn't come up with any new plan yet to convince her we should stay in Vermont, and now she was possibly going to see Mr. Jim again. I was stumped. Being stumped made me grumpy. I didn't feel like being nice to her.

It was after nine when I put my books and folders into my

backpack and set it by the door. Mama was watching TV on the couch.

"I'm going to bed," I said, heading toward the stairs.

She popped up. "Oh, wait, is there anything special you'd like me to bring back? Something for under the tree I might not have known you wanted?"

I could have left it alone. I could have done like we always did and told her something meaningless, like a new set of headphones or clothes. She loved it when I asked for clothes. But this time I didn't. Maybe the universe was pushing me in the direction I needed to go for the Stay-in-Vermont Action Plan to work. Maybe I was tired of pretending. Or maybe it was both.

"Nothing. And whatever else you got me, you should probably take back, because it won't be what I want."

"I do know what you want, sugar—"

"No, apparently you don't," I said, surprisingly composed. "I want to keep this farm. I don't want to sell it to Mr. Jim or anyone else. I need you to understand that I've never felt like I belonged *anywhere* until we moved here. I want you to know who I am, to understand the real me, the one who came to be after we got to Vermont. I know you thought giving me *things* instead of my daddy was right. I know you thought you were protecting me. I get that, Mama. But you were wrong. I needed him all along. You should have let me pick, and now it's too late."

I turned to go upstairs and left her at the bottom, holding

the banister like it was the only thing keeping her upright. About three quarters of the way up I heard a noise, like a tiny gasp. Or a whisper. Maybe it was wishful thinking. Or maybe I really did hear her say, "It was a mistake."

My stomach was in all kinds of knots in the morning, thinking Mama was planning to meet up with Mr. Jim. At lunch I snuck down the hallway to Deacon's office and slipped inside without knocking.

"Am I allowed to come in and ask you a question that isn't about school? I'm on lunch."

He shoved some papers into a blue folder and laid it on his desk. "You can ask me anything. Want to close that door?"

My throat was clogged as a Georgia highway. *Where to start?*

"Did you know Mama wants to sell the farm and move at the end of our year?"

"Not for sure, but it doesn't surprise me."

"Can she do that? I mean is she allowed to if I don't want to sell, since it's mine?"

He sat back in his chair and made a teepee with his fingers. "That's complicated. The short answer is yes and no."

"That's not an answer."

"Do you mean that's not the answer you want to hear?"

"You know what I want to know!"

"The trust is set up so after you've satisfied the obligation of living here one year, if you want to sell it, you can. That's not what your father wanted, but that's what he decided."

"But—"

He held up a hand. "I'm getting to it. I know you want to stay—I've seen it since that first time you went down to the sugar shack. Unfortunately, your mama can sell it regardless, with one caveat."

"What does that mean?"

"Stipulation."

"And?"

"Until you are twenty-one, I have to sign any sale papers, too."

"Because you're the trustee?"

He nodded. "Exactly."

"And you wouldn't, right? Because you know he wanted me to stay?"

"That's correct. I would not if I thought you were against selling it."

"So I'm okay? I don't have to worry?"

"Not about it being sold, if that's not what you want."

"That's all I want. What else is there to worry about?"

"Maggie, I have no guardianship over you. Until you're a legal adult, if your mama decides to move the two of you to Timbuktu or Alaska or anywhere else, there's nothing I can do to keep you here."

"Wait, she can make me move away even if we keep the farm?"

"Yes," he said quietly. "Even if you keep the farm."

* * *

That first night at the Parkers' I was miserable. Between the ruckus with Mama and what I learned from Deacon, everything looked gray and hopeless. Mama and I tiptoed around for two days before she went to Boston, each of us afraid to say something that would reopen the festering wound. When I got on the bus the morning she was leaving, she stood in the front window and watched it drive away.

That evening, I curled up on the big couch in the Parkers' living room and wiped tears away before they fell. Lucy scrunched her body close to mine and patted my arm. Biz sat on the floor and gave a running commentary of what was happening to the orphaned baby elephant on Animal Planet. James was working at the library. Kendra and Sonnet passed tape back and forth at the kitchen table, talking about the presents they were wrapping for the old people at the veterans home. Haily was trying to curl her hair in the bathroom and talk to Ethan Edward on the phone at the same time. She dropped the curling iron on her toe and squealed.

Lucy rolled her eyes. "The bf makes her so weird."

The house phone rang. I knew it was Mama because Kori took it into her bedroom to talk in private. She stayed in there half an hour, and when she came out she smiled at me like she was sorry about something.

Eventually, the concert of voices, the smell of homemade pies baking in the oven, and the way Kori touched the top of my head every time she walked by soothed my brokenness. When the baby elephant found a surrogate mother on TV,

Biz and Lucy flung their arms over their heads and cheered. The show ended with a clip of the grown-up elephant walking away across a savanna with its adopted baby trailing behind, as if no problem in the world couldn't be solved by a mother's love.

Kendra came from the kitchen and clicked the TV off.

"No more tonight," she said with authority.

Biz and Lucy wailed at the same time. It was hard to sort out until Kori came in and put a finger to her lips.

"It's the Jimmy Stewart movie night!" Biz cried.

"I know, you can watch it, stop fussing." Kori took the clicker from Kendra and the TV came back on. "We can break the rule. It's the first night of winter break."

Kendra rolled her eyes and marched off. Lucy pulled my head toward her and whispered, "Really, it's because you're here."

Over the next few hours there were bowls of hot chicken stew with fluffy little dumplings floating on top that we got to eat in the living room. James came home and plopped down at the other end of the couch to watch the movie with us. Haily went out with Ethan Edward. Kendra and Sonnet ran up and down the stairs at least a dozen times, collecting trinkets from the store to wrap. And Mama called again. Kori motioned to the phone held against her body.

"You want to talk to her?"

I shook my head and turned back to the television, where an angel had just gotten his wings.

THIRTY-SIX

"We only didn't get to go in the sleigh one time," Lucy said the next day. "And that's because it rained instead of snowed."

"Global warming," Kendra muttered.

"We almost didn't get to do it this year at all." Biz pointed to her head. "I mean, I don't think they'd do it if I was dead."

James buckled leather straps around Sassy's shoulders. Behind her was a shiny black sleigh that I was actually going to ride in to deliver presents to the veterans home.

"Biz, you would have looked down from heaven and told us to get on over there with the presents and pies, and you know it."

Lucy clapped mittened hands together. "After the old timers' home, we cut down our own tree!"

"Why do you cut a tree when you've got all those left over there?"

Kendra dumped a load of brightly wrapped presents into a canvas bag in the back of the sleigh. "Last ones. And we cut our own tree because we can."

"You weren't even here last year, so how do you know?" Biz chided.

"Yeah, how do you know?" Lucy repeated.

Kendra made mouthing motions with her hand and walked away. "Your parrots are squawking again."

Biz put her hands on her waist and imitated Kendra swishing her hips. "She and Sonnet think they're so cool."

Lucy held her hair out like Kendra's and wiggled. "So coooool."

"Okay, enough, both of you," James said. "Go tell the moms we're almost ready."

Biz bolted for the house with Lucy on her heels. "Wait! I want to tell them! No fair! Slow down!"

James watched them and smiled. "Lucy forgets there was a time when we didn't know if her sister would be here to run ahead of her."

He buckled the shafts of the sleigh to the harness, then clipped a string of gold bells to a leather strap across Sassy's back. Lucy and Biz scrambled into the backseat and pulled a heavy wool blanket over their laps. Sue and Kendra got in the Jeep and headed toward the road, followed by Kori and

Sonnet in the pickup. Boxes of pies were stacked in the back.

"Where's Haily?" I asked.

James pointed to the store. She and Ethan Edward stood in the window watching us leave. "They're in charge for the day. God help the customers."

"Ready?" Kori called out the window.

James gave her the thumbs-up, then motioned for me to get in next to him. "Lay that over yourself. It gets a lot colder once we start moving," he said, pointing to a red-plaid blanket.

He pulled one rein and clucked, telling Sassy to turn toward the road. The sleigh jerked and swerved when it first hit the ice. There was nothing even close to a seat belt to keep me from tumbling out the side, so I curled my fingers tightly around the seat cushion. Once on the road, the runners glided smoothly on packed snow. Sassy Pants's hindquarters bounced up and down with each step, making it look like the heart was dancing. The bells jingled and we whisked past bare trees glistening under the bright winter sun. Biz and Lucy giggled nonstop in the back.

We'd been moving along for a few minutes when James handed me the reins.

"Really?"

"Go for it," he said.

If I were still in Georgia, three days before Christmas, I'd be at the mall with Irene, the two of us buying each other meaningless presents with our parents' credit cards. I'd missed out on so much, not being here in Vermont with my daddy and the birch trees and the maple grove and the sugar shack and friends who loved me just the way I am. I'd never have seen the magnolia paintings, or heard my daddy's voice, or known people who said he was a really good man.

But for now, I was here. I took the reins and smiled so wide my teeth hurt from the cold.

James showed me how to pull the sleigh up to the front of the nursing home, where a uniformed man and woman stood at attention. James jumped out and saluted them one at a time before a pair of nurses eased the veterans into wheelchairs and rolled them inside.

Lucy raised her arms for me to lift her out. "Last year, this old man threw up all over Sonnet!"

"Yeah," said Biz. "And this lady kept yelling at him, 'I tell you every time not to eat the shrimp!'"

Lucy looped her arm through mine and pulled my ear toward her mouth. "Sometimes Sue and Kori fight, too," she confided.

We carried the bag of gifts to a table where Sue and Kori had already set out the pies. A gold menorah sat at one end, and a long, wooden block with green, red, and black candles was at the other. Seven words were carved into the wood: *Umoja, Kujichagulia, Ujima, Ujamaa, Nia, Kuumba,* and *Imani.*

Kendra came up next to me, holding a tray of tiny paper cups. "That's for Kwanzaa. They mean unity, self-determination, collective work and responsibility, cooperative economics, purpose, creativity, and faith."

"I like that."

"Yeah, so did my mother. Shame she didn't live by it."

She moved on with her tray of cups. An old man fell asleep in his wheelchair and spilled cider all over his pants. A lady knelt next to him and cleaned it up. "Oh, Dad," she said, then she dabbed a tissue where a smidgen of drool peeked from the corner of his mouth.

Sue waved me over when the pies were cut up. "Take two, pass them out, and come back for more."

"Who gets what kind?"

"Don't worry. They'll tell you exactly which one they want."

I took a slice of pecan and a slice of blueberry with me. The first man peered at them suspiciously and waved me away. "Come back when you've got mincemeat," he said.

A white-haired woman in a fuzzy blue bathrobe held both hands out. Her skin was thin as rice paper, see-through with brown spots.

"Thank you, lovey," she said. "I'll take two."

I looked back at Sue to be sure that was okay, but she didn't see me. The lady tugged on my shirt.

"Honey, I'm ninety-six years old," she said. "I served our country in two wars. I've earned a dozen pieces if I want them."

"Yes, ma'am." I gave her both and whispered, "Want me to find you some whipped cream?"

She smiled, but already had blueberry pie in her mouth

and couldn't answer. I went back to the table and got a piece
of the mincemeat for the man.

After everyone had pie and sparkling cider, a lady with
Director on her badge moved to the middle of the room and
clapped her hands to get everyone's attention. She had on the
ugliest Christmas sweater I'd ever seen. It looked homemade,
like someone had used up every drab color yarn they could
find to knit it for her. Even worse, little pieces of sequins
spelled out *Merry Merry* across the chest, and it was too
short. Every time she raised her arms, the sweater inched
above the waist of her stretch pants. Biz and Lucy could
hardly contain their giggles.

"I wrote this little toast last night," the director said. "So
don't anyone make fun of me. I'm not a poet, I just love all of
you."

She raised her cup and waited for everyone else to do the
same.

"To all who risked their life and limb, to serve us and pro-
tect, we thank you all with gratitude, and wish you all the
best."

"Hear, hear!"

"Happy holidays!"

"Merry Christmas!"

"Happy Hanukkah!"

Sonnet started up at the piano, soft at first, then louder
and faster until all the veterans rocked out to Christmas
songs. James carried the gift bag around the room. Old,

gnarled hands reached inside for the brightly wrapped packages, and within minutes, the floor was littered with red and green and silver paper. Strings of gold and white ribbon flew so fast we couldn't keep up with it, trying to stuff it all into trash bags.

I'd never seen people so happy over such simple gifts. No gold cuff links, no crystal champagne flutes. They got wooden puzzles, snow globes, pretend eyeglasses with bouncy Santas waving over their heads, and tubes of rose-scented hand lotion. Their eyes shone like little kids. They laughed and compared presents and traded until everyone was happy. It was a perfect, beautiful moment, and I didn't want it to end.

The blue-bathrobe lady put on a pair of oversize Santa sunglasses. "Looky here, lovey, I'm Mrs. Claus!" I went over to straighten them for her and she clasped her hand over mine. "What's your name?"

"Maggie," I said.

"Short for Margaret?"

"No, ma'am, my full name is Magnolia Grace. Magnolia Grace Austin."

She pulled her hand away and took the glasses off. "Magnolia Grace Austin. I thought that might be you. It's the accent that gave it away."

I stepped back, startled. "Do I know you?"

"Not unless your mother talks about me as much as she talks about you. I'm Freda. Freda from Alameda, that's what she calls me."

"My mother?"

"Isn't your mother Delilah?"

I nodded. "How did you know?"

"Honey, your mother is our favorite volunteer. Every Tuesday and Thursday, we can't wait for her to come!"

"Volunteer?"

Freda clasped her hands together and smiled. "She tells us the wildest stories, all about the places she's traveled, and why she decided on Vermont to raise you. I've never known anyone who has actually been inside the Vatican and got to tell a joke to the pope!"

"The Vatican?"

"And riding an elephant, as elegant as she is, who would imagine? Every time I think about her swaying side to side so much she got sick, I can't stop laughing."

"An elephant?"

Freda smiled like she and I had a secret. Behind me, Sonnet started playing "O Holy Night" on the piano, and the energy in the room shifted. The veterans' holiday party was winding down. Freda leaned forward in her wheelchair and placed her hand next to her mouth so no one else would hear what she was about to say.

"Mind you, Magnolia Grace, I'm not sure all her stories are true, but she makes us laugh and brings us joy, so at the end of the day, it doesn't really matter now, does it?"

THIRTY-SEVEN

"The only reason they had the Kwanzaa stuff was because of me," Kendra grumbled. "There wasn't one black person in that whole nursing home."

"If that's true, it's quite an honor," Kori said.

"It's not an honor. It's an obligation. People think they have to do it so I don't feel different."

"Um, hello, excuse me?" James raised his pant leg and exposed the titanium prosthesis. "Who is different?"

"Um, hello, excuse me?" Biz pushed her hair aside to show the curved scar James called her third elbow.

"Um, hello, excuse me?" Lucy had nothing to show except

the gap where a front tooth had fallen out that morning.

"Why do you always repeat everything everyone says?" Kendra snarled. "Don't you ever have an independent thought?"

She threw a box of tinsel on the floor and stormed from the room. I stood still and quiet, expecting pandemonium after her tantrum, but everyone kept decorating the tree as if nothing had happened.

We'd found the perfect balsam fir not too deep in the woods, and the whole house smelled like a forest. Sonnet unfolded layers of tissue and held up a homemade ceramic ornament of a horse and sleigh.

"You can tell Lucy painted this one—look at the pink dots on the tail."

"What's wrong with pink dots?" Lucy asked.

"Nothing," James said. "It's exactly the way Sassy Pants's tail looked after you gave her a glitter shampoo."

"She likes glitter!"

Biz scowled. "Not the day before my very first horse show. Everybody laughed at me!"

Lucy beamed at her mischief.

Sue came in from the kitchen. "Who wants fried worms for dinner?"

Kori's voice was right behind her. "It's not worm night, it's frog leg night. Straight from France!"

"Yeah, yeah, it's potpie, I already saw," Lucy said.

She twirled in place, wrapping braided gold ribbon around

her body, and giggling. Biz held the end and when Lucy was wrapped so tight she couldn't move her arms, Biz yanked. They both squealed. Lucy spun in circles until she toppled, landing under the tree.

James pulled her to her feet. "Careful, or you'll knock the whole thing over."

She wrapped her arms around his real leg. "Better look out or I'll tip you over!"

"No chance. I'm Titanium Man, remember?"

Kendra came back the same time Haily appeared, and the living room vibrated with bodies and tissue and ornaments and boxes and Christmas cards they hung from the wall.

"Don't forget, you have to put ornaments all around the tree," Haily said. She sounded unusually sweet. "We share the tree."

"What do you mean?" Kendra asked.

Haily pointed to the window and held a frosted crimson ball up. "When people drive by, they'll be able to see our tree from the road. We didn't spend all these years making ornaments to keep them to ourselves. Share, share, share."

James looked at her like she'd gone crazy and shrugged.

"What's wrong?" Haily asked.

"Nothing, we just thought you'd forgotten you had an actual family, that's all."

"What does that mean?"

Lucy climbed onto the arm of the couch, put her hands on her hips, and swished. "Because of Ethan Edward. You like him better and forgot all about us!"

Haily laid strands of tinsel over a branch. "You never forget your own family."

The phone rang. A minute later Sue motioned for me to go into the kitchen. "Your mom really wants to talk to you."

I took the phone and put it to my ear. "Hi."

"Hi, sugar, are y'all having fun?"

"Yup."

"Oh good, I'm so happy. I want you to know I've had great success. I'm glad I came."

"I don't even know what you're doing there," I said. *Except maybe digging up more Mr. Jims.*

"You'll find out soon enough. I'll be back tomorrow early afternoon. I'm bringing us something special for Christmas Eve."

She sounded so hopeful, like a little kid. I moved away from the door and spoke quietly into the phone. "Mama, are you volunteering at the veterans home?"

Long pause. "Why would you ask me that?"

"Because we were there today and I met Freda from Alameda."

Another long pause, then she laughed softly. "Oh, that Freda, she's full of fun stories. I'll tell you all about it when I get home, sugar, okay? I'll see you about two."

"I'm going skiing, so I won't be back yet."

"Skiing? Oh. Okay, sugar, have fun. Bye."

"Bye—"

223

Click.

Sue and Kori watched me hang up the phone. "Everything good?" Sue asked.

"I guess," I said. "Do you know what she's in Boston for?"

They looked at each other quickly. "It has to do with Christmas, so we can't tell," Kori said.

"But you'll like it," Sue added.

I'd never told them about Mama wanting to leave as soon as our year was up, because every time I was with them it was so easy to pretend nothing was wrong. Sometimes I felt jealous, because after I went home each day, they all still had each other. They were a family. A pieced-together one, but a whole complete family with two parents, sisters who got into fights, and a big brother with a leg buried in the backyard who let them climb all over him in a river. For a fleeting second I thought about Peter and Albert back in Georgia, sharing their first Christmas together, and I hoped they'd found with each other what the Parkers already had.

The noise coming from the others in the living room died down. Sue, Kori, and I went in from the kitchen. All six kids stood together, staring at an open box on the floor. Inside was a pile of polished wood ornaments attached to loops of thin leather. The magnolias. Their magnolias.

Kendra came to my side. "I don't have one either," she said. Not mournfully, not whiny, just a fact, as if this piece of news joined the two of us together in a way none of the others could share.

"That's because you weren't here yet," Lucy said. "If you'd been here, he'd have made one for you."

Biz dug her elbow into Lucy's side. "Shhh, you're not making it better."

Sonnet picked up the box. "You can hang these if you want."

"They're carved from one of the old maple trees," Sue said.

My brain tripped over itself inside my head, trying to make sense of the rawness billowing through me. James took a magnolia off the top, laid it in my hands, and placed my thumb on the smooth wood, streaked reddish brown, beautifully sculpted, and my daddy was there again.

"These are maple trees, our maple trees. They're almost as beautiful as magnolias, but they don't have a princess named after them."

One by one I hung the magnolias on the tree. Sue and Kori's were on the bottom of the box. I handed them to Kendra. "I should have given you more."

She hung the last two side by side, front and center. When she was done, we all stepped back and James plugged in the lights. The tree came alive with color and history like a rainbow quilt—like this family who had been brought together from the discarded scraps of other people's lives. I don't remember my heart ever feeling so full.

We drank tiny cups of eggnog sprinkled with nutmeg and ate miniature mince pies. Sonnet brought her keyboard into the living room and let her fingers bring music to our ears, music that made me feel happy, and safe, and loved. I was sure nothing could possibly penetrate the strength, the perseverance, the dignity of that evening in the Parkers' home.

"We belong here, Magnolia Grace," he'd said. *"We come from these woods."*

THIRTY-EIGHT

In the morning, delicate webs of ice crystals framed the living room windows. White lights above the door outside blinked off and on, and the reflection burst onto each streak of frost so they looked like miniature branches laced with tiny, twinkling stars. Snow drifted from the sky, soft and slow. For one short, delicious moment it felt like I'd woken up inside a snow globe, instead of on the couch in the Parkers' living room.

Biz and Lucy scrambled up and rocked the cushions. "It's Christmas Eve!"

Kendra rolled her eyes on her way to the kitchen. "Jeez,

give it a rest, would you? You'd think she was the second coming of Christ."

"Look what the toof fairy brought me!" Lucy held a silver dollar between her fingers and kept jumping.

Biz tugged my pajama sleeve. "We're going to give Sassy a hot bran mash this morning." Her cheeks were flushed, like she'd already been outside in arctic air. "When it gets cold really fast like last night, we have to give her bran so she'll poop."

Lucy giggled and rolled on top of my ankles. "Yeah, so she'll poop."

James waved from the kitchen and held out a Tupperware container. "Morning, Maggie. Girls, here's the stuff for the mash."

Lucy and Biz each grabbed the container and started a tug-of-war over who got to carry it outside. Haily ran into the room and crashed between them. Chunks of cut-up carrot, apple slices, and raisins scattered across the floor.

Lucy pushed both fists into Haily's stomach. "Look what you did!"

"Oh, get a grip. You're driving me crazy! Both of you. Which one of you took my curling iron for your stupid stuffed horses?"

Both girls shrugged, but the corner of Lucy's mouth twitched.

"I'm going in your room and if you take it again I'm going to burn your butts with it—" Her voice faded with the sound of her feet pounding up the stairs.

Sue appeared from the kitchen with a wooden spoon in one hand. A smile flickered on her face and she crossed her eyes. "Stop taking her curling iron!" She pointed the spoon at the girls and a glob of something white dropped to the floor. "Whoops! Morning, Maggie. Merry Christmas Eve, and welcome to the crazy house!"

Kori hauled a basket of clean laundry from downstairs. Under a red flannel shirt, she wore a T-shirt that read *I'm one of them!* across the front. "My dream house has a washer and drier on every floor." She set the basket on the coffee table and peered at me. "How'd you sleep?"

"Okay."

"Good. What time are you skiing today?"

I pulled the blanket over half my face and looked sheepishly at her. "I'm not. I didn't want to have to go home early."

"Oh," Kori said. "Well, I'll take that as a compliment."

Haily raced down the stairs, holding the curling iron like a weapon. "It's broken!" she screeched. "You two broke my curling iron and Ethan Edward will be here in five minutes! I'll never forgive you!" She disappeared again.

"Poor Ethan Edward, having such an ugly girlfriend with no curling iron," James said.

Biz and Lucy giggled. "Ugly girlfriend, ugly girlfriend!"

They ran to the door at the bottom of the stairs and tried to slam it, but Sonnet pushed through and shoved them aside. "Stop with the annoying stuff. It's Christmas Eve."

"Nonstop drama," Kori said. "Wouldn't have it any other way." She picked up the laundry basket and headed off down the hall.

"Water's boiling, you ready for the mash?" Sue called. The girls ran around gathering boots and hats and coats.

"I can't get my mittens on!" Lucy pulled and tugged and tried to wrangle her hand into the mitten until her face turned as red as the skin on the apple slices.

Kendra walked through with a plate of pancakes in one hand, a glass of juice in the other. "They're on the wrong hands, duh."

"Where do you think you're going?" Sue asked.

"To eat in my room, away from the heathens."

Biz waved her hands in the air. "Heathens! Heathens!"

"Heathens!" Lucy mimicked.

"See? They're giving me a stomachache."

"Back to the kitchen," Sue told her.

"Sonnet got to eat in her room for almost five months, all I want is one morning!"

Sue pointed to the kitchen "Go."

"Whatever," Kendra said.

"Biz, Lucy, wait downstairs. Out!"

All three girls disappeared. Sue let out a big sigh and smiled at me. "We'll be cleared out soon, don't worry."

"Where is everyone going?"

Kori stuck her head around the doorway. "Last-minute errands, but I'll be here for a bit. You can stay if you want."

I was barely awake. I needed time to think before Mama got home. I needed strength, perseverance, dignity, all the things that came from my name.

"You sure it's okay?"

"Of course." She went back to the basket of laundry.

Between the two moms, Sue was always good for a strong hug or giving directions to the masses. She wasn't the one I'd automatically go to for tender words like I would Kori. But this morning she changed the rules.

"I know you're not happy at home right now, kiddo," she said softly. "But it'll be okay. Cross my heart. Promise." She drew an imaginary *X* across her chest.

"It'll be okay," he'd said. "Cross my heart. Promise."

He'd made an X over his chest with his fingers, set me on the stone wall, and kissed my cheek. I'd believed him. I had no reason to think anything else. So, I'd stayed on that wall until the stones grew cold, and the light faded to strange shadows, and unknown voices called my name.

THIRTY-NINE

Kori handed me a plate of pancakes with a blueberry happy face on top. "What time is your mom getting home?"

"Two, I think."

"Well, good. We can have a leisurely breakfast then." She dipped a triangular piece of pancake into a little cup she'd microwaved with her syrup and butter mixed together.

"Your dad's syrup is the best. He gave us enough to last until the little girls are in college."

"Did you ever watch him make it?"

"Oh yeah, every year. He was a really good friend, not just

to me and Sue but to the kids."

"Did he have other friends?"

"That's a tricky question. He wasn't one to go out and seek friendships, but he was well regarded in Vermont. Beloved, even."

Beloved.

"And, he was instrumental in Sonnet's progress when she first came. That's how we got to be close."

"What do you mean?"

"When Sue and I first bought the store, we only had Haily and James. They were little, under ten. We'd filed to become adoptive parents, then social services called one day and asked if we could foster an emergency placement. Sonnet came that night, barely six. I'll never forget. She was in a pink dress and half the lace around the bottom was ripped. She had different shoes on each foot, those huge brown eyes, and no voice."

"She couldn't talk?"

Kori shook her head. "The night before she came, she was sitting in a booth at a Denny's and watched her father out the window getting carted away by the police after a drug deal. There'd been a lot of commotion, so one noticed her for a long time. She still freezes when she hears a siren, and she won't go near fireworks. CPS said the lack of speaking would be temporary, until she felt safe again, so we went about the business of making that happen. We put all three kids in bed with us every night, kept her with us night and day. The first time he saw her, your dad was smitten. He stopped by every day to check on her, and told her stories about a little princess named Magnolia Grace."

"About me?"

She nodded. "He drew pictures for her, too. It fascinated Sonnet to watch his hands. I turned around one day and she was sitting on the floor with crayons everywhere. She'd gotten a box off the shelf and was coloring the wood."

"Wow."

"Yeah. That's when she started carrying crayons around in her pockets all the time. Now it's a pencil. Then one day your dad didn't show up. Deacon told us he'd gone for some treatments in a hospital. We tried to explain to Sonnet, but she shut down, so we gave her stacks of paper and all the crayons in the store. She colored frantically and constantly, and saved everything in a shoe box."

"Do you still have them?"

"She has a few. Your dad looked different when he came back. He'd put on some weight and his energy felt lighter, easier, more peaceful. When Sonnet saw him, she got that shoe box and gave it to him. Then she smiled really big, and you know what happened?"

Kori hesitated, trying to find her voice. I waited, silently.

"She spoke for the first time since she'd come to us. She handed him her pictures and said 'Magnolia Grace,' plain as day. Her first words were your name."

Everything I thought I knew about Sonnet changed in

that second. Her silence, her frantic sketching, the way she kept her distance from me but told Aspen and Jane I was brave. It all made sense.

"I never thought she liked me."

Kori laid her hand over mine. "She doesn't dislike you, Maggs. She still struggles to speak. Your dad taught her to use art to help with her anxiety. They had a special bond. Not like you and he would have had, but for Sonnet, it was a saving grace."

She watched me carefully.

"Do you think she doesn't like me being here?"

"I think you came so soon after the accident, and you look so much like him, it's been hard for her. But even if her distress feels directed at you, it's not. It's about what she lost."

Before I left, Kori handed me a brown bag with some presents in it for Mama and me to open the next morning.

"One last thing," she said. "The same way Sonnet's grief isn't about you, neither is yours truly about your mother. Think about that before she gets home."

FORTY

Eleven o'clock. Three hours until Mama would be home from Boston. Three hours to be at home alone and try to figure out the next step in what had become a huge mess between us. I tucked myself onto the window seat and watched white flakes drift from the sky. Only two days in and I already loved winter.

Outside, red and brown cardinals flew to the suet feeders. They clung to the wires and pecked at Nut N' Berry and P'nuttier blocks. Sometimes one of the feeders would get crowded, causing a fight to break out. They settled their squabbles with a lot of sharp screeching, then went back to the business of eating.

The clock ticked slowly. By eleven twenty-seven I'd been up and down from that window seat a half dozen times, pacing to the kitchen and back, opening and closing the front door, knocking icicles from the overhang on the porch, putting a kettle on the stove for tea, then turning it off because I didn't really feel like tea, then climbing back onto the window seat. Nothing I did made the roller coaster inside me calm down. Only the peace of the snowy woods and the sugar shack would help clear my head.

Unbroken snow came halfway up my calves and filled my boots. It didn't matter. The woods were tranquil, and except for the buck who moved gracefully away when he saw me, they were all mine. That first day, when I'd stumbled upon the maple grove by chance, the shack was almost hidden by vines so tightly wound around the door, I'd barely been able to squeeze inside. In the fall, a carpet of scarlet maple leaves blew in and covered the brick floor. Today, snow swept past frosty windows and weighed down pine limbs, so the view was solid white over a bough of green.

If I could bottle up the scent of snow-covered pine, mixed with the sweetness of leftover maple sugar still clinging to the inside of those cauldrons, I could take it with me anywhere. Wherever Mama moved us, I would have these woods with me forever. I sat at the table and ran my fingers over the initials. I missed my daddy. Even without ever really knowing him, I missed him.

My fingers traced the *J* and the *A* and the plus sign. Then they followed the pattern of the *D* and the *A* and the equal sign. Only after those came the *M* and the *G*.

Mama's love for him came before mine. Like Sonnet, she'd loved him, too.

Shadowy arms reached for me. I was afraid. He hadn't come back like he'd promised. He'd left me alone. Strangers said he wasn't feeling well, he'd gone to the doctor. They'd carried me home through the woods to Mama, who ran down the field, her arms stretched out, palms up, her face red and wet from tears. She grabbed me and held me so close I could feel her heart beating against mine.

FORTY-ONE

At ten till four, my finger hovered over Mama's speed-dial number on my cell phone. I paced by the window, watching the driveway for a glimpse of red through snow that fell in heavy waves. Mama wasn't a cautious driver already, but with this storm—I didn't want to think about what might happen.

The TV news mocked me with images of multiple cars piled on top of one another after skidding off the highways. Reporters switched to their "tragedy is upon us" voices and used words like *treacherous* and *catastrophic*. I raced to the family room, flipped off the TV, and threw the remote against the fireplace, then ran back to the front door to keep watch.

Finally, the red Mustang swished back and forth up the driveway, narrowly missing the big oak tree. I yanked the front door open. A gust of wind blew snow across the front porch and into the hall. The Mustang swerved and swayed before stopping close to the steps. Mama got out and made her way carefully to the house, leaving the car engine running.

I held the door for her, surprised to see her eyes shining. Snowflakes clung to the ends of her lashes. Everything about her vibrated. Without a word, she discarded her coat on the chair, stomped her boots to shake off the snow, then took me by the elbow and led me to the couch.

"I was worried," I said. My voice sounded so tiny.

She put her hand against my cheek. "I'm sorry, sugar, I was afraid you might have tried to call me. I dropped my cell phone in the snow and it took me so long to find it, I think it's ruined. I couldn't call out. But that doesn't matter. Everything's going to be okay."

She took both my hands in hers and squeezed.

"Mama, I—"

"Shhh, let me talk first. I know you're angry and sad and everything else in the world, and I don't blame you. I made a mistake. The way we lived in Georgia, it wasn't right. I thought what I was doing would make you happy and would keep you safe. I should have known that wasn't what you needed. You're so much like him. I'm trying to make up for it now, sugar, I'm trying to give you what's left."

She wouldn't let go of my hands, like Lucy when we crossed the field to the river a lifetime ago. My heart thumped in my chest. The front door opened and a gust of wind blew through the house before it closed again. I looked to the hallway.

"Who's here?"

Mama shook my hands. "Look at me, sweetheart, right here. These are people you need to meet. This is the best I can do, the closest I can get you to your daddy."

Deacon led a small man into the room. An even smaller woman followed close behind, trying not to trip over Quince, who ran excited circles around them.

"Quince! Stop!" Deacon sounded nervous, sharp.

"Are they my relatives?"

"Not like you mean, but Mr. McCarthy is related to your daddy in another way."

Deacon got them settled in the wing chairs facing me and Mama. Quince stopped running and sat by the man's side. He patted the top of her head.

"You're a good dog, yes, you are, a good girl—you know, don't you?"

They turned to look at me, but no one said anything. Nothing. Not one word. Forever.

The woman had a round head, and even rounder chipmunk cheeks with circles of pink on the top of each one. Even her hair was a mess of mad brown curls framing her face.

Mama went to stand in between the two chairs so all three of them could stare at me.

"Well," said the man. "You are Magnolia Grace, and I am Cornelius McCarthy."

"Yes, sir."

He gestured to the woman. "This is my wife, Jenna McCarthy."

In Georgia, I would have stood up and crossed to shake their hands, but my legs were shaking so hard I didn't know if they'd hold me up. Deacon brought in two suitcases and took them directly to the guest room.

"I don't mean to sound rude, but you're all making me nervous," I said.

"Nervous?" asked Mr. McCarthy.

"I'm sorry, sir, but I don't know who you are."

He took his wife's hand and they smiled at me. "Your mother went to a lot of trouble to get us here."

Mrs. McCarthy's voice sounded like a bird chirping. Each word ended on an upward note.

"Your father saved my husband's life, Magnolia Grace. We came to say thank you."

"Were you the people in the car when he was killed?"

"No, sugar, the McCarthys never met your daddy."

"Then how, what—"

Mr. McCarthy stood up and took off his long navy coat and yellow sweater. He handed them to his wife and sat down again. Mama watched from between the two chairs.

Spiderwebs of black mascara spread all the way down her cheeks.

"Magnolia Grace," he said. "When your father passed away, he left this farm to you, but he left something to me as well."

His fingers slowly unbuttoned his shirt. It was like some crazy dream where strangers act like they know the very heart and soul of you and behave in ways that would never, ever happen in real life and you can't talk or move away.

He opened the shirt a crack, just enough for me to see a raised red scar running all the way from his collarbone to the middle of his torso. Another smaller one went left to right about two inches below.

"I didn't meet him in person, but he still saved my life. Your father was an organ donor." He tapped two fingers on his chest. "And, inside here, is his heart."

I watched the fat, ridged scar rise and fall. The only sound in the room came from the puttering of Quince's breathing as she slept by his feet.

"We waited two years," Mrs. McCarthy said. "Every day we prayed, every day we waited for the perfect match. Finally, we got the call. Your father, Magnolia, he gave us the gift of my husband's life when he lost his own."

I pointed a finger at the scar. "You mean my daddy's heart, his real heart, is in there?"

"Right in here," Mr. McCarthy whispered. "Alive and beating."

Mrs. McCarthy stood up and led me to the chair next to her husband. After closing his shirt, she laid my palm on his chest, over where they'd opened him up to put my daddy's heart inside, so one of them could live.

"Can you feel it?" Mr. McCarthy asked.

He'd put my tiny hand on his chest. "Can you feel it?" I'd nodded, but it wasn't true. I couldn't feel anything except soft hair and warm skin. "My heart will always beat for you and your mama."

"Not really," I said. "I want to, but I can't."

"Give her the stethoscope, Jenna. We bought a toy one so you could listen."

I plugged the pieces into my ears and Mrs. McCarthy slipped the little silver circle under Mr. McCarthy's shirt. At first, the sound was soft and far, far away. Mrs. McCarthy pushed a little harder, and then I heard it. Ba-boom, ba-boom, ba-boom. He was coming back for me. Ba-boom, ba-boom, ba-boom. His heart. My daddy's literal heart was still alive, still beating. Just like he'd promised.

I listened to that beautiful sound and let tears fall onto Mr. McCarthy's shirt. I could have stayed like that forever, hearing my daddy's heart beat, remembering his strong arms that would never let me fall, and the way he smelled of grass and paint and Listerine, and the gentle lilt of his voice when he said "I love my girls."

Behind me, Mama finally let her real emotions bubble out through tears and sobs and spurts of laughter and sniffles. I knew she was sorry, and she'd done the best she could. And I knew she'd found this man and brought him here on a snowy Christmas Eve so I could hear my daddy's heart. She didn't have to say it out loud: she'd done it all because she loved my daddy, and she loved me. I leaned down and put my mouth up next to Mr. McCarthy's chest.

"Hi, Daddy," I whispered. "It's me, Magnolia Grace."

FORTY-TWO

Brilliant yellow sunshine spilled through the windows on Christmas morning. Almost two feet of new snow sparkled in the field, as if someone had dropped a million perfect diamonds from the sky. I itched to escape down to the sugar shack, but I wasn't the only one up early. Mrs. McCarthy and I built a fire and watched the flames flicker and curl around dry pine logs. The sweet scent made the noises in my head finally rest.

I tucked myself into the window seat so I could see the birds outside at the feeder. Mrs. McCarthy sipped tea and watched with me. She understood I didn't want to talk. Not yet. It was all too new, too fresh.

A little after nine James showed up with a box of pies and an invitation to dinner.

"Those people, the McCarthys, they're still here," I said. "That's a lot of extra people to cram into your place."

"This is true," he said. "One sec." He turned away and punched numbers into his phone.

I carried the box to the kitchen. Inside, stacked one on top of the other, were blueberry, buttermilk, and mince pies, all with perfect, crinkly crusts around at the edges. Wedged in between was a handwritten note:

We tried to remember which was your favorite, but decided you liked them all. Here's a sample pack to get you started. Merry Christmas, Maggie and Dee! Love, the Parkers. ♥

James came back with Deacon. "The moms said we can make it work there, or we can bring the dinner here."

"Over here? Yeah!"

"Don't you want to ask your mama first?" Deacon said.

"We were going to eat Chinese because in all the excitement, Mama forgot to plan anything."

Mrs. McCarthy came up behind me, her cheeks puffed up like two tiny pink rosebuds. "The Chinese was my idea. I'm Jenna McCarthy. You must be one of Kori and Sue's children."

"Yes, I'm James."

"Well, James, the others are still asleep here, but I'm an expert in problem solving, and I think that's a lovely idea. Now," she said, scanning the kitchen and living room. "How many people are there?"

James counted with his fingers. "Fourteen including Ethan Edward."

"Do we have folding tables? We'll need two. Eight-footers. Magnolia, how many chairs are there here? We won't need side tables—those kitchen counters go on forever, and we've got that oak table by the window. We can serve ourselves buffet style. James, what will your moms be bringing?"

As tiny and timid as she'd seemed at first, Mrs. McCarthy organized things like a boss. By one o'clock the sofa and wing chairs had been pushed against the walls, and two long tables covered with red, green, and gold plaid cloths took their place in the family room. Mix-and-match china and silverware made up fourteen places. Leftover centerpieces from the tree lot sat in the midst of dozens of tiny tea candles.

Mama was all aflutter. When she found out "her girls" were coming, she coated her eyelids with bright-blue shadow and put that awful sparkly stuff in her hair. "It's their favorite," she said.

At one ten, Biz and Lucy raced in, tracking snow all the way to the family room.

"Mrs. Baird!"

"Mrs. Baird!"

Mama scooped them into her arms.

"Look what we got for Christmas! *Charlotte's Web*! Let's read it together!"

Lucy held out the same book I had upstairs, the one that had been home to my daddy's picture all those years. Mama oohed and aahed, then leaned in close to them. "Only if you do one thing for me first."

Two little people stood side by side, shoulders touching, eyes glued to Mama's face, waiting, hoping what she would ask was manageable.

"I'm not Mrs. Baird anymore. You can pick what you call me. Auntie Dee. Delilah. Mrs. Austin. Grandma, although it would be kind of a miracle to have a grandma younger than your own moms, wouldn't it? But you pick. Then I'll read."

She sat down on the bottom of the stairs and folded her hands in her lap. Biz and Lucy whispered to each other, then looked at Mama.

"Okay, we decided," Biz said.

Lucy shoved her with her shoulder. "Quiet. I get to say it!"

"Then say it!"

"We want to call you Elizabeth Taylor."

"Elizabeth Taylor?"

"Yeah. The moms told us you were prettier than her."

"We didn't know who she was, so they showed us a picture and she was almost as pretty as you, but not quite."

Mama looked over to where Sue and Kori stood in the kitchen and blushed. "Your moms said—oh my goodness, well, what a lovely name, I don't think I could have thought of one I like better myself. Elizabeth Taylor it is, then! Now, come sit with me. I think we have time for a chapter or two before we eat."

FORTY-THREE

We had roast goose for dinner. I'd never eaten roast goose, but it came out of the oven moist on the inside and crispy on the outside. Sue held her hand over Biz's and let her "carve" the breast. When she proudly held up the first dark, juicy piece, everyone cheered.

I ate foods I'd never heard of before. Creamed chestnuts, some kind of puff pastry with lobster and a pink champagne sauce inside, chunks of grilled root vegetables served with bowls of nuts—which Kendra explained symbolized the African harvest—potatoes mashed with so much Vermont cheddar cheese they turned orange, and cranberry sauce that didn't start in a can. And pies. The Parker family did love their pies. But the best part was the delicious, happy noise that filled the house from bottom to top.

Before dessert Mama tapped her glass with a knife. "I want to thank all of y'all for making this the merriest Christmas ever. And I want to especially thank the McCarthys for letting me bring them from Boston and giving such a gift to Magnolia."

The McCarthys blushed and mumbled something about not having kids of their own.

"In the excitement of all y'all coming, I forgot to give Magnolia her real gift." She held out a flat, rectangular package, decked out with a silver bow and shimmery streamers draping end to end. "Open it, sugar."

Thirteen pairs of eyes watched while I tore off the paper. Fourteen, if you include Quince. Inside was a giant book of maps. One page for each of the fifty states. My heart sank to my feet.

Mama saw the look on my face. "Open it up."

My hand shook as I turned to the first page. An index.

"No, go to the first state. What's the first state in the alphabet?"

"Alabama!" Biz cried out. "Look at Alabama!"

"Quiet—you don't even know what's going to be there," Haily said.

Alabama had been marked with a black X across the whole page.

"Go to the next one," Mama said urgently.

"Alaska!" Biz yelled.

"Shhhh." James clamped his hand over her mouth, but she wiggled out.

Alaska had a big, black *X* through it, too. So did Arizona, Arkansas, and California. Every single page had been crossed off, all the way through Utah.

"Vermont's next! We're next!" Biz could barely keep her bottom in her chair.

My fingers cramped when I turned the page. No black *X* crossed off Vermont. Instead, about three quarters to the top and slightly right of center, was a hot-pink sticky note with an arrow pointing to a tiny green dot. In Mama's handwriting the note read *We live here!* followed by a little happy face.

I couldn't even look up. Salty tears drenched the entire state of Vermont. My shoulders shook so forcefully I almost dropped the book. Mama laid her hand on the back of my neck, and pressed her cheek against the top of my head.

"I do understand you," Mama whispered. "It took me a while, but I do."

Once the electric moment had passed, after I'd blown my nose and washed my face, after everyone had settled down and talk of dessert buzzed, Mama said there was something else.

"Y'all know I loved working at the store that day—I had so much fun. And I love spending time at the veterans home with Freda and all of them. But I want to go to college. It's

253

always been my dream to study fashion design. But it's not right for me to live off the money your daddy left you, sugar. That should pay for your college, and whatever else you want. I've talked this over with Deacon, and with your permission, I'd like to lease out part of the farm."

"Lease it to who? For what?"

"Mr. Jim is interested in a twenty-year lease of the maple sugar factory. He would rent all but one hundred acres. That would give us enough money to live on so we could stay here, in the house, plus add a little more to your college fund."

"What about Peter? He said he'd always look out for us."

"And I'm sure he would. But wouldn't you rather cut ties with Georgia and be on our own?"

I looked at Deacon. He gave a slight nod. "That's why he kept everything all these years, so you could decide yourself what to do with it. If leasing out the factory his father built means you get to stay here, I have no doubt he would approve."

Everyone leaned forward in their chairs, waiting. Mama's hand rested on my back. Her bright-blue eye shadow had faded, most of her lipstick was gone, and mascara smudged into half-moons under each eye. What was left was the most beautiful future-fashion-designer face in the entire state of Vermont.

FORTY-FOUR

After dinner I put on my parka and mittens and snuck out to the front porch in search of quiet. It was a lot, all the stuff happening inside. I needed to think about what it meant that we'd get to stay. My cheeks ached from smiling all afternoon. It was the best kind of ache.

The front door opened and Sonnet poked her face out. "Do you need to be alone?"

"I'm okay. You can come out."

She sat down beside me and handed me a brown document folder tied shut with a string.

"I want you to have these. Your dad made them."

Inside were four colored-pencil drawings: a mermaid, a

kitten with a girl's face, a princess, and a magnolia bloom.

"I don't know what to say. These are yours, he gave them to you."

She shook her head. "They were always meant for you. I was just the guardian."

I rubbed a finger across the mermaid's face. "Does it make you sad to give them away?"

"No. I was there when he drew them. You didn't get that part. That makes me sad."

I thought about that for a minute, that I'd missed things like watching him draw mermaids and tell stories. But if we'd stayed when I was little, he would have been a different father than the one I'd come to know. There'd probably be no Deacon, no Quince, and no Mr. and Mrs. McCarthy. He wouldn't have gravitated to Sonnet and helped her get well. In the end, Mama might have left anyway if she hadn't been able to cope with his brokenness.

I carried the folder through the woods as carefully as I imagined a person carried a newborn baby. Sonnet and I had just passed through the birch grove when something jumped out of the snow. I jerked to a stop, but it was gone.

"Did you see?"

"Shhh," Sonnet whispered. "Watch."

A bump in the snow trailed away from the hole where it had disappeared. White powder flew into the air again, and two black eyes popped out. Black eyes and a pink nose darted left, then right, then got sucked away again.

"What is it?"

"A winter ermine."

She put a finger to her lips. The ermine shot up again like a bullet, spun around in midair, and dived headfirst into the snow. He was solid white except for the tip of his tail, which looked like it had been dipped in black paint. Sonnet pointed to a mound moving away from us.

"He's under there, making that ridge."

"I've never seen an ermine."

"You probably have," she said. "They're brown in the summer and turn white in the winter."

"He was so cute."

"People think they're so cute they make coats out of them. It's disgusting."

I turned away and started through the woods again, wondering if Sonnet had ever seen Mama wearing her fur coat. Maybe now she'd put those kinds of things away. The things that she'd used to fake her way through a tough time, along with all the Georgia rules that had no place in Vermont.

It took both of us to push enough snow away from the door to the sugar shack so we could squeeze inside. Sonnet stopped in front of the fireplace and looked around the room.

"I've haven't been here since he died," she said.

"I love this place. This is where I started to learn about him."

"Did you know I was there, at the accident?"

I nodded. "I'm sorry."

She turned away so I couldn't see her face. "It was so fast. He took me to Middlebury to see an exhibit of his art. He didn't usually go, but the moms said he was trying to reach out. You know, be more active in the community. On the way home we stopped to help those people. He told me to wait for him, but he never came back."

I shuddered. She stood straight and tall. Her long black hair tumbled from under a fuzzy blue hat.

"You're the only person I've ever said that to out loud. Maybe you'll be a shrink someday." She turned and sat at the table, tracing the carved heart with her fingers.

"You can still use the piano if you want."

"Are you sure?"

"I'm definitely, positively sure. He'd want you to."

She tipped her head a little. "Yeah, he would. Thank you."

I leaned against the wall and inhaled deeply. "I love the smell in here. Maple syrup and smoke. It smells like home."

"Are you going to make syrup in the spring?"

"I don't know—I wouldn't know what to do."

"Deacon does. He still carves spiles from birch wood. Those are what go into the tree so the sap runs into the buckets. Johnny Austin didn't like metal spiles, so Deacon keeps a bucket of sticks in his house and whittles them."

"Did my daddy make syrup this year?"

"He died just before sugar season. It's usually close to the first day of spring."

"So is my birthday."

"I know."

"Why does Deacon keep making spiles?"

"He said in case you wanted to make syrup. But really I think it's because it helped him not be sad."

"Like the way you do art, and the way I run?"

"Yeah, like that."

I could barely see through the windows for all the frost covering the glass, but right outside were hundreds of maple trees my daddy had made syrup from for years.

"Is it hard to make?"

Sonnet shrugged. "It's not my thing, but it's not hard. Takes time and someone who knows what they're doing. Deacon's done it his whole life."

"Then we should make it, right?"

"That's up to you. It's your farm now."

"It's my farm now." I touched my cheek. "It really is."

Wind blew through a gap in the door. I handed Sonnet the folder and ran out to an opening between the maples. The trees waved frosted branches, losing their shine as daylight waned. Casting my arms to the side, I fell backward and landed softly in a bed of fresh snow and made my very first angel. When I was done, Sonnet was outside sketching me. And she was smiling.

By the time we got back it was nearly dark. The whole house was lit up, and new candles Mama'd bought in Boston flickered in each window. Sonnet and I walked wordlessly across the field, breaking a new trail. It was okay being with her—she didn't talk nonstop like some of the others. We could be quiet together.

From outside the kitchen I could see all the way to the family room. A bright fire glowed, and the lights on the mantel twinkled. Deacon stood beside the fireplace with Quince at his feet, watching the rest of them play charades. Mama was in the center of the room, flanked by Biz and Lucy, making odd gestures with her hands and laughing. I'd never seen her laugh that way before. Every few seconds one of the girls whispered to her and she made new awkward motions until everyone in that room was in stitches.

Mr. McCarthy leaned over and kissed Mrs. McCarthy. Haily and Ethan Edward were stuffed together in the window seat. James sat on the stairs, his fake leg stretched out in front of him. Kori and Sue shared a floral wing chair, and Kendra sat cross-legged in the other. Even she was smiling.

"The moms got approval to adopt Kendra. They told her this morning."

"No wonder she's been happy all day. She's lucky."

"We're lucky, too," Sonnet said. "You and me. Even in our unluckiness, we're lucky."

I looked at the people playing games in the family room, all of them brought together by a bit of luck and the strangest of circumstances, like a hodgepodge quilt that had been stitched together by the one person who was no longer here.

The familiar warmth started at the top of my head and spread down my neck, through my heart, all the way to my toes, and his voice cradled me again.

"Family, Magnolia Grace. A beautiful, perfect family."

Acknowledgments

Every story that resides within us must wait for a completely innocent happening to unlatch the door that sets it free. There is no knob you can turn, no key, and no button to push to gain access. There is only the magic of a split second when something triggers the release of a story that must be told.

After reading a short essay by Frederick Buechner in a class I was taking a few years ago, Magnolia Grace and the Vermont setting slipped out that door and landed on the piece of paper I had been using to take notes. I wrote the beginnings of this book during class that evening. Many thanks to my insightful and patient teachers, Brian Nystrom and Becky Strout, and to all my EFM classmates for your understanding and encouragement.

The journey of this story was revealed to me through the words of a friend who offered an emotional testimony about a job she'd had as a fundraiser for pediatric heart patients, work that resulted in three children receiving life-saving heart transplants. Thank you, Clare Payne Symmons, for sharing that special time in your life with someone you barely knew, and for always seeing in me what I cannot.

To my children, Parker and James, who still have no idea how much my love for them influences the hard work that goes into writing a novel. It is for you that I will never, ever quit. ♥

Love and gratitude to Bettina Whyte, who graciously offered me sanctuary and creative space within her beautiful home. Your friendship and love shine throughout this book.

To my high school friends Carol (Hurley) Hemphill and Karen (Murphy) Rochelli, who swooped in to rescue me when I was lost, even though we hadn't seen each other in more years than I care to put on paper. There are not enough words to express my gratitude to you both, and to Carol's husband, Ron. I can't wait for the next reunion.

I am forever indebted to Kelly Hatch and Kathy Flickinger, who allow me the freedom to be creative and crazy during the workday. Thank you for supporting my writing, and for listening to me wade through plot points and scenes while counting crickets.

To my loyal friend and supporter Ruth Boggs, who makes me feel like maybe I do actually know what I'm doing. You are such a blessing.

This book is also for The Real Biz, who spoke the honest and innocent words from which many of these characters were born.

To my superhuman editor, Andrew Harwell, whose

brilliant and thoughtful vision and guidance turn my chicken scratch into something beautiful, and all the hardworking and uber-creative folks at HarperCollins, thank you, thank you, thank you.

I will forever be amazed that my agent, Al Zuckerman, the legendary founder of Writers House, plucked me off the streets and agreed to represent neurotic and needy me. Thank you for always having my back.

And last, but far from least, so many thanks to the powerful women who understand the value of shenanigans. Never would I have found my way without your guiding lights, your words of wisdom, your prayers, good juju, and all things brass. I love you all.